Black Dog
&
Other Gothic Tales

by Icy Sedgwick

Other books by Icy Sedgwick

The Grey o' Donnell Series
The Guns of Retribution
To Kill A Dead Man

Short Story Collections
Checkmate: Tales of Speculative Fiction
Harbingers: Dark Tales of Speculative Fiction
Black Dog & Other Gothic Tales

The Magic & Mayhem Series
The Necromancer's Apprentice
The Necromancer's Rogue

Before We Get Started

If you enjoy this book, please take the time to leave a short review at whatever retailer's site you purchased it from. Reviews help other readers find good books!

You can also get an exclusive short story collection from my website – but more on that at the end of the book.

Buckle in, keep your arms inside the car at all times, and enjoy the ride!

For the Muse. It's nice when she shows up.

Contents

Black Dog

My name is Samuel Phipps and I offer my position as a clerk within a firm of engineers as testament to my sanity. I can offer no other evidence as to the veracity of the events which I am about to relate, other than the testimony I shall lay before you.

I was staying with my brother in a small Norfolk village; he has been recently married and I had promised to visit with him and his dear wife. On the night before I was due to take my leave, bound once more for London, I had been visiting another friend on the edge of the town. My brother could not make the visit due to illness, and I found myself in a position of having to leave my friend's lodgings without arrangements for transportation being made.

It is not so large a village that one feels compelled to travel by coach, or even horseback, and at that moment in my visit, both were extravagances which I could ill afford. I deemed it prudent to make the short journey on foot, and took my leave of my gracious host. Moments before I left, he offered the suggestion that I might shorten my return journey by some ten minutes or so by cutting through the graveyard, instead of following the meandering lane. I thanked him for his suggestion, and stepped out into the cold March air.

I had not gone three paces when a small hand tugged on my arm. I am not accustomed to frights, or extended indulgence of my imagination, but the suddenness of the act startled me. I looked down and saw that the hand belonged to that of my friend's maid. She had been returning to the house from the chicken coop when she heard my friend's suggestion, and she begged me to ignore the advice, and take my intended route. I told her that I wished to return home and if my friend's suggestion would allow me to do so all the quicker, then I would follow it. She told me that the graveyard was the haunt of the infamous 'Black Shuck', and she pleaded with me to take the longer route, "all the better to avoid 'im". The little maid seemed convinced that my soul would be lost should I encounter the beast, seen only in the graveyard on nights such as these, and I saw no way to placate her that would not involve a lie. I assured her that I would take the long walk instead, and left her clasping her hands in gratitude.

I am not a man prone to such notions, but I regretted my choice the instant I set foot in the graveyard. A narrow gate admitted me in the rear wall, and a winding path cut a swathe between a host of stones. I normally find such places to be fascinating records of human experience, but with a cold wind at my back, and frost in the air, I found I had little time to read the stones. I fancied I heard footsteps, yet when I turned my head, I saw nothing in the moving shadows.

Something howled in the darkness behind me, and I glanced over my shoulder to discover its source. The path was empty. I heaved a sigh of relief and turned back to the path ahead.

A large black dog blocked my way. Around three feet high, it stood perhaps seven yards away, with ragged fur and enormous paws. Red eyes burned in its impassive face, its features akin to those of a mastiff. It did not snarl, or bare its teeth as I feared it would. It regarded me with vague interest, but I sensed no real malice on its part. I recalled the fevered words of the maid and wondered if this was the Black Shuck of which she spoke. I found I could not move, bound to the spot as I was with fright.

The dog walked along the path towards me, carrying itself with the dignity one more associates with cats than dogs. It regarded me all the while with its red eyes, and I could not even close my own to prevent my seeing its approach. Some nefarious agency kept my eyes wide open. The dog sniffed my hand in the manner of any normal hound, and lifted its gaze to meet my own. I saw nothing in its eyes, no danger or evil, nor wilful defiance of the Lord. The dog simply...was.

With no warning, it stood on its hind legs, and pressed its paws against my chest. I would have started for I felt no weight behind the gesture, no sudden movement that may cause me to stumble backward. The dog gazed into my eyes, and let out a single bark. An instant later, my eyes closed and I regained control of my limbs. When I opened my eyes, the dog was gone, and I was alone in the graveyard.

I hurried home, and arrived at the same moment that I surely would have done had I taken the longer route. I did not tell my brother or his wife of my ordeal, and I retired to bed, pleading a headache. I did not wake for two days, and when I finally did awake, my brother's wife explained in halting terms that the coach I was to have taken overturned on the journey, killing its occupants.

I returned to London a day later, somewhat fearful of the coach, and discovered that a fire destroyed my lodgings on the day I should have returned. A host of such tales played out before me, and soon my acquaintances congratulated me on my run of good fortune. I smiled and shook their hands, agreeing in turn, but I could not bring myself to speak of the events in the graveyard, nor tell of the two mysterious marks that had appeared on my chest, marks shaped like those of cloven hooves.

A Woman of
Disrepute

I always made a point never to visit artists while they were working on a painting but, given the chosen profession of a large number of my friends, it often happened that I had no choice in the matter if I wanted to see them. That desire for companionship in the face of tedium explained why I found myself standing in the doorway of Henry Woollenby's workshop, waiting for an invitation to sit. No invite was forthcoming, nor did I feel it would be so in the immediate future, so I hung my hat and coat on a stand by the door.

"So this is what you called me to see? What is it?"

I walked across the room to view the vast canvas that dominated the narrow end of the wedge-shaped workshop. The painting depicted a misty scene on the banks of the Thames, and globules of fog clung to the lamp posts in the distance. The black waters of the river lapped at the edge of the beach, low tide having deposited the body of a young woman on the dirty sand. Blackfriars Bridge loomed to the west. Henry darted about in front of the painting, dabbing a spot of paint here, or a streak of oil there. I wrinkled my nose.

"Henry, why must you persist in painting such morbid subjects?"

"I believe it to be reality. I seek only to paint the truth." Henry did not look up from his work, but I considered myself fortunate to have received a reply at all.

"The truth? What is true about what you've produced?"

"Isn't it obvious?" Henry paused, and turned away from the painting. I should have been repulsed, but I could not avert my eyes from the pale, outstretched arm of the fallen woman, her fingers curled as if to beckon me closer. I wanted to know her plight, what sorry state of affairs could have drawn her to such an ignominious end.

"No."

"This is a regular occurrence, my friend. These women do not fall from grace, they are pushed! What happy ending can they possibly hope for in such a world? Their only salvation lies in the Thames."

"I could not agree more, but do you have to paint pictures of it?"

"Is that not the duty of art? To 'make glorious' that which the greater public would rather ignore?"

"The duty of art is to bring beauty into the world. It is simple decoration, and nothing more—you cannot pretend that art's function should be that of moral instruction. No, you should leave such lofty ambitions to writers and orators," I said.

"Writers like yourself, I suppose?"

"Indeed, writers like myself! We may use language to communicate, and narrative should be our preserve, not yours."

Henry snorted and returned to his work. I peered

over his shoulder, examining the background as his brush flickered in and out of my field of vision. A dark stain within the shadow of the bridge caught my eye, some sort of hooded figure with its head bowed, facing toward the dead prostitute. A shiver ran down my spine.

"Who is that?"

Henry stopped and followed my pointing finger. He frowned as he bent closer.

"I have no idea."

"Did you not paint it?"

"I don't know. I don't exactly remember. Perhaps I did so late one evening as my senses departed for the night. Yes, that must be it. That may be the personification of guilt, or shame, felt by the women themselves."

Henry nodded and, apparently satisfied by his own explanation, resumed painting once more. I raised an eyebrow, my gaze fixed upon the hooded figure.

"Did you actually see such a thing when you were there?"

"When I was where?"

"Down by the river. At low tide?"

Henry's ears flushed red, and he refused to turn around. He bowed his head, his brush sagging in his hand.

"You didn't go down to the river, did you?"

Henry shook his head. I raised my eyebrow.

"And this is not a scene you painted as you found it, is it?"

Henry shook his head again. The red flush crept down the back of his neck and disappeared beneath the collar of his paint-stained shirt. He'd protested so often about the veracity of art. It simply confirmed my assertions that truth is the preserve of the writer.

"Don't tell anyone, but I've never even spoken to an unfortunate. They terrify me. I'd heard the stories, and seen what the other chaps were painting, so I had the daughter of my charwoman pose for the woman."

I snorted. "It hardly makes this a painting of truth, does it?"

Henry said nothing. He resumed painting, his brush slower and more lacklustre than before. He continued in this fashion for several minutes, until it became clear that conversation would be strained at best. I shook my head, and stood.

"I can see that you are busy, so I shall leave you in peace. I assume we will all see you at Dawkins's supper on Friday?"

"That you will, Edward."

"Excellent. Until then, goodbye, my friend."

I closed the door behind me and descended the three flights of stairs to the front door. I exchanged pleasantries with the charwoman as she washed the front steps, and made my way into the thick fog of the London night.

* * *

The image of Henry's painting remained in my thoughts as I walked, and I compared it to the works I had seen at the Academy, reminding me of a discussion with that infernal Dante Rossetti about fallen women. Snippets of prose tugged at my attention, and my senses tingled with the promise of a new story. I snorted again at Henry's belief in the moral obligation of art. No, if anyone were to expose the public to the horrors of street life, it should be me.

My feet took me in the direction of Southwark. My publisher's brother-in-law had told me of a less-than-reputable club in the area, and advised that I 'sample the wares' if I wanted a higher standard of female company. I had no intention of doing such a thing, but the idea of a new muse loomed large in my mind. My last had left London two weeks ago to marry an industrialist in Birmingham, and we had all heard tales of Rossetti's circle finding their muses in the most unlikely of places. Why might I not find a new one in the bowels of the Virginia Club?

Red lamps adorned the club's tables, and corseted

waitresses served drinks to men hidden in shadow. I took up a seat near the door, reluctant to venture too far inside lest I find it difficult to find my way back out, and ordered a glass of sherry. Within moments, a blond beauty appeared at my side.

"Is this seat taken?" She gestured to the empty seat.

"Not at all." She sat down and I admired her graceful poise. A pile of golden curls sat on her head, although several ringlets had escaped their pins, and lay against the girl's pale neck. I tried to picture her standing alone on Blackfriars Bridge, contemplating her fate as she stared into the churning black water below. Yes, she would do.

"I'm Ellen," she said.

"Edward Bonneville. Pleased to make your acquaintance."

She smiled and leaned forward. I tried to guess her age, which I placed at between seventeen and twenty-three. God alone knew what she'd done for employment at this establishment.

"I shall be honest with you, Ellen, I am not looking for the sort of companionship one might find in a place such as this."

"Oh." Ellen's smile evaporated and her gaze began to wander the room.

"No, I seek a muse, and I suspect you may be exactly what I'm looking for."

The smile returned, as did her attention. I suppressed a smirk—Ellen had no doubt heard tales of women elevated from the lower classes through their association with artists and writers, and sought a similar advancement for herself. Henry's painting again came to mind and my inner smirk faltered. Perhaps I could prevent another tragedy.

"What do you want a muse for?"

I explained my position as a writer, though disappointment rankled me that Ellen had not heard of my work. I told her about Henry's lofty ambitions, and my desire to tell the truth that he could not, and in the course of my narrative, I described his painting.

"It's common enough. Girls get too old or sick and men don't want to know. They can't make any money, so..." Ellen allowed her words to hang in the air but the unhappy conclusion was plain enough to infer.

"It's very sad, but I feel literature could do so much more than art."

Ellen nodded, as if she knew what I meant. I remembered the hooded figure.

"However, there was something a little unsettling about Henry's painting, and I don't just mean what it was about. No, there was a hooded figure in it that Henry didn't remember painting."

The colour drained from Ellen's face and her fingers curled around the edge of the table. Her knuckles turned white and a muscle worked in her jaw.

"The girls fear something worse than the loss of their virtue, sir."

"What do you mean?"

"Oh nothing!" Ellen pasted a false smile on her face. She stood to leave, her hands trembling as she knotted her fingers together.

"Where are you going?"

"I'm sorry, sir."

Ellen disappeared into the gloom of the club. I rose to follow her, but the shadows swallowed her, leaving me with only darkness for company. Two men near the door cast suspicious looks in my direction, and I hurried out of the club and into the cold London night before questions could be asked.

Once outside, I thought again of the peculiar conclusion to our conversation. Ellen spoke of fear, yet refused to divulge the contents of her thoughts. She evidently believed I could offer no aid in the face of some nearby danger, yet I could only speculate as to the nature of this threat. Perhaps one of the local men was to blame, growing fat on the profits of the female bodies he sold, and keen to threaten them if they chose to leave.

I wandered the streets for around half an hour, where I passed furtive men on their way to the Virginia Club, and gentlemen heading home after late-night visits to friends. The hook of a story nagged in my mind, and I found that I turned in the direction of Blackfriars Bridge. As I walked, I turned the topic over in my mind. I wanted to give the fallen women a voice, but I could only do that by speaking to them myself and hearing their stories with my own ears. I needed affirmation of my suspicions about a shadowy underworld figure, intent upon ruling the unfortunate women with a rod of iron.

I approached the bridge in search of another muse, but I spotted blond curls farther up the street. I peered closer and realised they belonged to Ellen. She hurried towards the bridge, her hair loose around her shoulders. She darted glances in all directions as she walked, her arms drawn tightly across her chest. Her boots beat an irregular rhythm in the quiet street as she varied her pace. She was clearly terrified of something. Maybe if I took her somewhere warm and gave her a drink, she might speak. Indeed, I was shocked to see her alone in such a place so late at night, and after her sudden fright at the club, I was concerned as much as I was curious.

"Ellen!"

Ellen stopped and turned. Recognition sparked on her face, but her expression was unreadable. Before I reached her, someone stepped out of the darkness of the alley to Ellen's left. Ellen turned and threw her arms up in a defensive gesture, but a pale hand shot out of a dark cloak and covered Ellen's mouth, cutting off her scream. I broke into a run but Ellen was dragged into the alley.

I reached the narrow lane. I expected to see her skirts bunched around her waist, or the flashing blade of a knife in the gloom. Instead, a hooded figure bent over Ellen's prone body, obscuring her face. Wet, sordid chewing sounds filled the air, and my stomach churned to hear them.

"Hi there, stop!" I found my voice, but it bore a waver that betrayed me. I tried to move into the alley, but my feet refused to obey. They held fast, rooted to the spot, while my knees quivered from the exertion of my run. My heart pounded, and my ribs vibrated within my chest, though from terror or exercise I could not say.

The stranger stood. Blood clotted in the bite marks around Ellen's mouth. The figure leaned down and held its hand—a horrible skeletal hand of bleached bone, over the wound. It tore upwards in one savage motion. For a moment, a white mist, the same shape and form as Ellen, hung from the figure's grasp.

"You there!"

The creature, for it was no human, ignored me, and folded the white mist into a neat square, which it tucked into the folds of its cloak. The figure bent down and caught hold of Ellen by the shoulders. It dragged her out of the alley, and up the quiet street. Shock gripped me, yet somehow it did not surprise me in the least. I did not question this peculiarity, consumed as I was by my desire to help Ellen. I struggled to move in order to follow their progress, but my feet refused to obey my commands. I pummelled my thigh with my fists, helpless and frustrated. My mouth kept moving, my vocal chords straining to cry out, but no noise would come forth. It was as though I were trapped in that terrible sort of dream in which you can see the world moving around you, but you are powerless to intervene.

As the apparition reached the approach to Blackfriars Bridge, my feet broke their bonds. The sudden movement impelled me to stumble forward, hurrying along the pavement towards the unholy pair. Revulsion at the sight raged inside me and I no longer thought of the story that I had originally sought to tell. I sought only to better understand what was happening. I ran towards the bridge, where the monster reached the mid-point. It hoisted Ellen up onto the stone balustrade, and her body tumbled into the freezing waters below. I cried out in despair.

The hooded figure wiped its hand on its cloak, and free of its burden, it drifted towards me. I stared, straining my ears for the sound of footsteps, but there were none. I shouted something nonsensical, I know not what, and while I saw no eyes, I was aware of the weight of its gaze. The malice that this figure bore for me was as apparent as the sensation of winter in December. This was no normal man, ruling and punishing the unfortunates of London. This was something else entirely. The apparition, belonging to some awful class of spectre previously unknown to me, continued down the bridge and turned onto Southwark Street.

I stood in the street, my feet pointed towards the bridge but my body twisted in the direction of the creature's exit. I wanted to recover Ellen's body, but I would surely perish in the cold waters, and that would simply add an extra tally to the creature's card. I had a notion to call for help, but only a priest could help poor Ellen now, and there was naught the constabulary, such as they were, could do. Part of me wanted to turn tail and flee, to run back to my rooms and avoid late night excursions into London's bizarre streets. Yet despite the animosity that the figure clearly displayed towards me, another impulse wanted to follow it, to make sense of what I'd seen, and to quiet the rising voice inside me that sought answers. As I struggled to decide upon a course of action, another voice added its tones to the clamour, raging about what a fine story this would make.

I could not turn myself away once my feet began walking. I kept the infernal creature in sight, and hurried along Southwark Street. My quarry sped on, although I did not think it knew I was following—unless it knew that I was on its trail, and did not care. Indeed, having seen its manner of murder, I scarcely believed that it would consider myself to be a threat of any kind. I wondered if I had perhaps seen a wraith of some kind. Indeed, I remembered the novel of Dr Polidori, *The Vampyre*, and speculated that perhaps this was the manner of their feeding.

The creature darted down another street, and I paid no attention to where I was. I kept thinking of Ellen, the beautiful, tragic blonde dumped into the Thames with cruel abandon. Even if she became nothing else, she could have been my muse. Now she would be another sentence or two in the newspaper, a mere footnote to the country's mistreatment of unfortunate women.

I followed the figure along Redcross Street. It reached a pair of iron gates, and drifted between the bars. I approached the gates some moments after, and found them fastened with a large padlock. I grasped the bars, pulling on them with all of my strength to determine the means by which the creature gained access. There must have been some way through to which I was not privy, although I suspect my desire to discover a rational explanation was my mind's defence against the fantastical events to which I had borne witness. I peered between the bars into a simple yard, moonlight falling across its uneven cobbles. The monster made its way toward the centre.

"Hi there, you! Yes, I see you!"

I shouted through the gates. The creature paused at the centre of the yard and turned its head in my direction. An angry hiss filled the yard as it lay down on the bare ground, and melted into the cold night air.

I stared between the gates but there was nothing to be seen. It had simply disappeared. I continued to stare as though it may yet reveal itself, as though the trick might be explained through rational means.

I could not allow myself to believe that a being capable of lifting a young woman over a bridge could pass through iron bars and vanish into the cold night air as though it did not exist. An idea flitted through my mind that I had dreamed the entire thing. Perhaps lack of sleep, or a morsel of undigested dinner, had played tricks upon my eyes.

"'Ey up, what are you doin' here?" A gruff voice interrupted my thoughts.

I turned around to see an elderly man grasping a staff in one hand and an ancient lantern in the other. A moth-eaten watch cap perched on his balding head, and a tattered cloak did its best to keep out the chill of the night.

"I was just looking for someone. At least, I thought I was."

"You won't find no one in there, sir," replied the night watchman.

"I thought I saw someone go in."

The watchman frowned. He peered between the bars, and looked down at the padlock. He raised his gaze to meet mine.

"No way to get in, sir."

"I saw someone, I am sure that I did." I peered into the yard, and turned my gaze back to the night watchman. A chill ran down my spine, and I shoved my hands into my pockets.

"Tell me what 'appened, sir?"

I told the watchman about my quest to find a muse, and my need to tell the story of the fallen women. I explained about meeting Ellen, and about what I saw in the alley. I realised the folly of my actions, but the tale poured out in a jumbled rush, and I trailed off into silence when the watchman started nodding.

"I know who you saw."

"Who?"

"I don't know 'er name, but I know 'er lives in there," said the watchman, pointing into the yard.

"This weren't always a yard. Many years back, this was a burial ground, yes it were. Only it weren't fer no usual folk. This was fer the geese of Winchester."

"The what?"

"The street women what was put to work by the Bishop of Winchester. They was called his geese. The one what you saw...she's the grand old mother, ain't she? When you saw her bendin' over that girl, she was takin' her soul. She dumps 'em in the Thames so the running water can wash away their sins."

"She does what?" If the watchman had told me such a tale yesterday, I would have called for a policeman and recommended he be taken to Bedlam, but after the events of the evening, I found I was incredulous although not entirely disbelieving.

The night watchman repeated his words. I stared at him, eyes wide and unblinking.

"You expect me to believe that a former prostitute, dead for centuries, is taking the souls of fallen women, and dumping the bodies in the river? I thought they were committing suicide."

"No, sir. It's the Mother Goose. She takes 'em. Frees 'em from a bad life. You know 'er cloak? It's the cloak of all 'er sin when she were alive. She's been quiet for a while, dunno what's prompted her to take it up again."

"I see."

"I reckon yer would be best off goin' home, sir."

I nodded and moved away from the gate, casting a last look into the yard before I walked away down the street. The night watchman waved as I turned the corner. I believed it to be only my imagination when I saw the faint outlines of the street through him.

* * *

The following morning, I browsed the newspaper over breakfast, immersing myself in society gossip and business news until the events of the previous evening seemed naught but a bad dream.

A knock at the door disrupted my reading. I glanced at the clock on the mantelpiece—only eight o'clock, yet I expected no visitors at such an hour.

I opened the door. My landlady stood in the hall-way, flanked by a policeman and a well-dressed gentleman. I clung to the door, my knees suddenly weak. I had done no wrong, but the sight of a policeman at one's door is apt to cause discomfort of some kind.

"Yes?"

"Are you Edward Bonneville?" asked the gentleman.

"I already told you he is," said the landlady.

"I just need sir to confirm this, madam." The gentleman's tone was light but firm. He gave her a pointed look, and she pursed her lips.

"If you need me, I'll be downstairs." The landlady hobbled away along the corridor. The third step down creaked, and I assumed she had stopped on the stairs to eavesdrop. Unless I took action, the contents of our transaction would be spread around the parish before lunchtime.

"Perhaps you'd care to come inside?"

I held open the door and gestured for the men to enter and they shuffled inside. I sat in my threadbare armchair, and offered its twin to the gentleman. The policeman took up a position near the door, hands clasped before him.

"Yes, I am Edward Bonneville. What can I do for you, Mr...?"

"Inspector Abbott. I just have a few questions for you, Mr Bonneville, shouldn't take too much time. First, could you confirm your whereabouts yesterday evening?"

"I went to visit my friend, Henry Woollenby. He's an artist, and he wanted me to see his latest painting."

Inspector Abbott nodded to the policeman, who

fished a notebook out of his pocket and scribbled down Henry's name.

"What else did you do, sir?"

"I came home, Inspector."

"I see, sir. Did you do anything in between? Did you perhaps visit another establishment on your way home?"

Inspector Abbott stared at me, his gaze pinning me to my seat. A lie withered and died on my lips, and I sank into the chair. It was no use pretending anything other than the truth.

"I did swing by the Virginia Club for a spell."

"Did you talk to anyone while you were there?"

"Yes, a lovely young woman named Ellen. I was doing some research—I'm a writer, you see, and I wanted to get some first-hand impressions to enrich my latest work. I realise it's not the most salubrious club in London, but it was on the way home and it was recommended to me." I ignored the policeman's sneer.

"I see, sir. And did you see this Miss Ellen after you left?"

"Not at all, Inspector."

"It's a pity you say that, sir. Only I have it on good authority that you did see the lady later that evening. Does Blackfriars Bridge ring any bells for you?"

My stomach clenched and an icy weight coiled itself into a knot in my gut. I opened and closed my mouth several times as I fought to find the right words.

"I know what you're getting at, Inspector, but it's not what you think. I did not kill Ellen, and I certainly didn't throw her body in the Thames."

"Ah, so you know what became of her."

I fell silent. Any lies would be useless now as I had given myself away.

"If you didn't kill her, then who did?"

I studied the inspector's face. He had a warm countenance, and a kindly expression that encouraged me to trust him. I sat forward in my chair and spilled the story in an uninterrupted flow. I told him about the hooded figure, the one from Henry's painting, and I described my pursuit of the creature to the old yard. I recounted the night watchman's words, even explaining the figure's strange garb.

"What a to-do! I've never heard anything quite like it."

"Yes, I realise it sounds bizarre, but it's the truth. Go and find the old watchman, he'll back me up."

"We'll do just that, sir. I'm sure he can clear all of this up in a jiffy. One question though, if this creature doesn't like you, why hasn't it done anything to you yet?"

"I do not know. I have asked myself that as well but...I just do not know."

"I see. Well will you excuse me? I just need to speak to my colleague here, double check his notes."

The two policemen ventured into the hall, leaving the door ajar. I leaned forward, straining to hear their conversation. Only snippets floated through the crack.

"I think he did it alright...oh I know he believes all that rubbish...clearly insane....Bedlam."

I leapt out of the chair like a cat on a hotplate at the mention of Bedlam. No, I would not spend my days in a madhouse for anyone. I searched the room for proof of my innocence, but all I found was scribbled notes from the night before. I could not even read some of my writing, so desperate was the scrawl.

"We'll have to get permission..."

Even in my state of panic, I recognised that I had to get away. They would not seek out the night watchman, so I would be forced to do so myself. With his testimony, they would see I spoke the truth, and all would be well.

I hurried to the window, slid the sash up and crawled out of the gap. The yard lay two storeys below me, but the kitchen roof provided a platform of sorts to my right. I inched along the window sill and jumped across the narrow gap to the sill of the neighbouring room. Flakes of lime wash peeled away from the sill, coating my feet.

"The window!"

The inspector's voice floated out of the open window, and his head poked out into the cold morning air. He looked across at me, his kindly expression grown hard and unyielding.

"Stop!"

I threw myself into open space, and landed on the kitchen roof with a thump. Dazed and winded from the fall, I rolled down the roof and into the yard. I cried out when my knee made impact with a misshapen cobblestone. I looked up and Inspector Abbott disappeared from the window. Shouting came from inside the lodging house.

I forced myself to my feet and made my way across the yard. The back gate stood open, no doubt left unlocked by the coal man, and I limped out into the alley. I hurried towards the street, half-dragging my left leg behind me. My head start gave me just moments to disappear into another alley before the two policemen reached the yard.

I plunged down one street after another, ignoring the stinging cold, and the stares drawn by my flapping dressing gown and mad gait. The morning fog stung my eyes, and I hurried onward, ever mindful for the sounds of commotion behind me.

My stupor cleared when I reached Blackfriars Bridge. The usual throng of people parted as they steered clear of my unusual attire and air of desperation. Two figures remained still, unwilling or unable to move with the crowd. I peered through the fog, and recognised the hooded figure from Henry's painting. My vision cleared and I recognised her companion. The night watchman. He pointed to me while speaking to the creature, and I found I could read his lips.

"He talked." The night watchman knew that I had spilled her secret. Or, rather, their secret. He told me to dissuade me from pursuing the story further, but now I had passed it on. The creature set off toward me.

I turned to flee back in the direction from which I had come, thinking even Bedlam would be preferable to a final encounter with the Mother Goose, but my feet refused to obey. I opened my mouth to shout for help but no sound came forth. Panic fluttered in my mind, turning my thoughts to ice as I struggled to move. I was as frozen as I had been the night before, during the attack upon Ellen in the alley.

The figures advanced. I squeezed my eyes shut but still they came toward me. The night watchman brandished a club, and the hooded figure drew back her sleeves with skeletal hands. I ravaged my throat with silent screams. The hooded figure pushed back her hood. My mind imploded at the sight of the naked skull, and the fires of vengeance burning deep inside the empty eye sockets.

* * *

Inspector Abbott scanned the report one last time. The body of Edward Bonneville had been pulled from the river, and the coroner recorded a verdict of suicide—believed to be prompted by guilt. The inspector frowned as he read of the mysterious bruising around Edward's head and shoulders, apparently caused by some form of heavy blunt instrument. The vocal chords were tattered, and bite marks were found around his mouth.

The inspector stood and threw the report in the fire. He placed his mother's rosary in his top pocket, and left a new report on his desk, one which made no mention of bruises and bite marks.

This latest story was the final straw. It was time to pay a visit to Redcross Street.

Midnight
Screams at
Holborn

A haunted tube station wasn't where most men might spend their Saturday night, but Simon Villiers didn't run with the crowd. At least that's what he told himself as he sat on the bench by the stairs on the eastbound platform. It sounded better than the actual explanation—that he really needed the money.

The Evening News lay on the bench, the headline proclaiming the appointment of a new chancellor in Germany, a strange Austrian fellow with a mad stare. Simon moved back and forth in front of his photograph to see if the eyes followed him. After a few minutes, he leafed through the paper and found the same advertisement he had answered several days earlier.

Do you believe in ghoulies and ghosties and long-legged beasties, and other things that go bump in the night? Dare you spend the evening in a haunted station on the London Underground? Are you man enough to withstand the horrors of the tube from dusk until dawn, and survive to tell our readers about it? If your answer is yes, apply to our offices for the chance to win £30!

The reward money had caught Simon's eye more than anything else. £30 would buy an engagement ring, and leave plenty to put towards the exotic honeymoon Marnie deserved. The dare seemed like an easy way to earn the money; he believed in ghosts, but found the idea that one wandered the British Museum tube station just too far-fetched.

The man at the Evening News had given Simon a pamphlet before he descended into the station, waving for the assembled photographers. He examined it now. The emergency exit routes were printed on one side, at the request of the station manager, while the other side bore tales of the ghost Simon should expect to see. He knew why, of course. The newspaper wanted to implant ideas about the ghost so that he would see it in every shadow, hear it in every sudden knock or tap. If he left before dawn, they wouldn't have to pay up and they'd get a ghost story in the bargain.

"That's not going to happen to me, nope, not at all!" Simon cringed at the hollow sound of his voice as it echoed along the platform.

Simon stood and jammed his hands into his pockets. He had the full run of the station, from the platforms up to the ticket halls, but he was under strict instructions to stay off the tracks. The station master had assured him that no trains would come through the station tonight, and the cleaners had already been and gone, but Simon had no intention of going anywhere near the tracks. He was badly paid, not stupid.

With no particular route in mind, he strolled along the platform and headed up the stairs; he wanted to stretch his legs. He passed a battered green door, probably some sort of storage cupboard. Or was it? Simon remembered what Davey had said that morning, when he'd told him about the bet. Davey had assured him there was a secret tunnel up to the British Museum itself from inside the station. What better place to hide a secret tunnel than somewhere mundane and nondescript, like a cleaner's store?

Simon grabbed the handle and pulled, fully expecting it to be locked. Instead, the handle gave way and the door flew open. Mops and buckets clustered in the sudden pool of light. He peered into the darkness, and a black stain detached itself from the shadows at the back, reaching its arms towards him. He stumbled backwards, and peppered the air with expletives as the figure pounced.

"Hello, darling!" She threw herself at him, arms outstretched. Her familiar voice jolted his nerves, and he sucked in a deep breath.

"Marnie! You scared the life out of me!" Simon's heart thudded as he folded his girlfriend into a hug. He gave her a squeeze, more to ground himself than give her comfort.

"Oh, I'm so sorry! I thought I'd hide in there until everyone left but then I lost track of time. I didn't realise how late it was until you came in." She pulled away and closed the cupboard door.

"What are you doing here?" He had never told her where he was going that evening, just that he couldn't see her. She'd find out once the story made the papers, but by then he would hopefully be £30 better off and able to propose.

"Davey told me where to find you, and I couldn't believe you'd agreed to do this without me!" replied Marnie. "What fun, eh? The night in a haunted station!"

"I'll kill him when I next see him. I'm supposed to do it alone."

"Don't be silly, Simon. You're far less likely to run away screaming if I'm here, and when we make it to dawn, you can claim that money." Marnie gave him a meaningful stare, and Simon was torn between pride and disappointment that she'd worked out his plan.

"How will you get back out without being seen?"

"A girl has her ways, dear. Anyway. Has anything happened? Did I miss anything good?" Marnie looked around her, as if a ghost might choose that exact moment to wander through a wall.

"Not yet. All quiet on the Western front, as they say."

"Oh, that is a bother."

Simon smiled. Even though Marnie wasn't supposed to be there, he was glad she was.

"I thought I might have a stroll around every hour or so," he said, leading her back to his bench. A satchel sat on the floor beside it. He'd packed a flask of coffee, some sandwiches, and his copy of Aldous Huxley's *Brave New World*. Simon thought a futuristic novel might make him less likely to see ghosts everywhere.

"Ah, great minds think alike!" Marnie held open her own bag, and Simon laughed when he saw the contents. Another flask of coffee, another package of sandwiches, no doubt ham and cheese, and another book—this time, William Faulkner's *As I Lay Dying*. She'd also brought a pair of torches, and something else—a board of some kind.

"What's that?" asked Simon.

"I told Bella what I was doing and she said that it might be a good idea."

"You told Bella? No one is supposed to know you're here!" Simon saw the prize money disappear in a puff of smoke.

"She's my sister, Simon! She won't tell anyone.

Besides, she's not supposed to have this, so we're even." Marnie pulled the board out of the bag, and Simon whistled. He'd only seen pictures of them, but there was no mistaking the neat rows of letters, or the words 'Yes' and 'No' written in faux-Gothic script in the corners.

"A Ouija board? Really?" he asked.

"If there is a spirit down here, then we can find out why she's here, or what she wants. She must get dreadfully lonely. I know I would."

Simon grimaced. He didn't mind spending the night in a supposedly haunted station, but he drew the line at wasting time on a séance. His friends told stories about terrible things that had happened after using the boards, though they'd only ever heard of them "through a friend". Simon dismissed it all as nonsense. He'd been to a séance before the previous year, and the board had mostly spouted gibberish. The only question it got right was answering what year it was, and even then Simon was convinced Davey had pushed the planchette himself.

Marnie put the board on the bench beside her and then unscrewed the lid off her flask to pour herself a cup of coffee. Simon fished out his own flask and did the same.

"Here's to a night of ghost hunting!" Marnie held up her cup.

Simon knocked his cup against hers, toasting the evening with coffee. He drank quickly, wrapping his fingers around the cup to steady his hands. He'd never spent a whole night with Marnie before. What would people say if they found out she was down here with him?

"What did anyone tell you about the ghosts?" she asked after she'd drained her cup.

"I was given this," replied Simon, handing over the pamphlet, "but everyone just focuses on the Egyptian princess. How many ghosts are there?"

"Mostly people just talk about the princess, but I've heard all sorts of stories. Most stations have at least one ghost. Wouldn't it be fun if they walk the tunnels at night, and pop up in each other's stamping ground? I suppose they must get dreadfully bored otherwise. Wouldn't you?" Marnie pouted.

"The pamphlet says you can hear the screams of the princess all the way down the tunnel at Holborn," said Simon.

"Is that so?" Marnie glanced at the pamphlet.

"I haven't heard anything, and I use Holborn a lot. Mind, I haven't heard anything here, either."

They passed the next half hour telling each other ghost stories as they wandered around the station. Marnie was a treasure trove of tall tales, gleaned from evenings with "the girls", while Simon relied on the snippets he could remember of the stories his grandfather had told. There was only one story he didn't tell her, about that fateful October night in 1917, when his grandfather had answered the door to find his son, Simon's father, on the doorstep. He wouldn't come in, but smiled at him, and disappeared right in front of his grandfather's eyes. Simon was only nine then, and in bed at the time, but he understood well enough when the letter of condolence arrived a week later.

"Simon darling, I'm awfully bored." Marnie sat on the bench, kicking her shoes against the tiled floor.

"I'm sorry, I don't know what else to do. We could have a picnic?"

"I'm not really hungry yet."

"We've both got books."

"I'm not really in the mood to read."

Simon was about to reply that he could suggest other things for them to do, but that he wasn't sure they were 'proper' activities for a deserted tube station, when Marnie picked up the Ouija board.

"Come on, old boy, let's give it a go!"

"Old boy? I'm only a month older than you." Simon stuck out his tongue. Marnie waggled the board at him, and Simon rolled his eyes. He had no real reason not to, and even if nothing happened, at least it might while away another half hour.

Marnie slid off the bench to sit on the floor, arranging her legs beneath her, and set the board on the bench. She moved the planchette to the centre and placed the tips of her middle fingers on its edge.

"Come along, darling. You should do the same."

"I'm sure you need more than two, dear," said Simon, sitting on the floor beside her.

"Oh stop being such a spoil sport, it'll be fine," said Marnie.

Simon settled his middle fingers lightly on the planchette, copying Marnie's pose.

She waited a few moments for silence to descend, and spoke. "Oh Egyptian princess! Can you hear us?"

Simon peered around him, torn between wanting nothing to happen, and wanting to see an Egyptian princess walk through the wall towards him.

"Spirit? We only want to speak to you. We mean you no harm."

Still no response. Marnie tried for ten more minutes, alternating between pleas for an audience, and trying to cajole the elusive princess into an appearance. Simon's legs fell asleep, and he shifted several times in an attempt to will life back into them.

"Marnie, I don't think this is going to work."

"I don't understand why nothing is happening. I've done everything properly."

"Maybe she just doesn't want to talk to us, love."

Marnie took her hands off the board and slumped back. She pouted at the unmoving planchette then pushed herself to her feet.

"Aren't you supposed to close the board first?" asked Simon, a dim recollection of the last séance rattling around his memory.

"I don't think you have to if no one speaks to you."

Marnie wandered across to the platform edge. Simon stood up and followed her.

"So what do we do now?"

"Let's have that picnic you mentioned earlier."

They turned back to the bench, and Marnie gasped. The planchette now indicated 'Hello'.

"Did you do that, Simon?"

"No. It was on the eye at the top when I got up."

"Are you sure?"

"Yes. Positive."

The planchette slid up the board, coming to rest on 'Yes'. Simon could see the whites of Marnie's eyes, and his own mouth hung open as they watched the planchette trace out a message on the board. It spelled 'You should not be here'.

"Why not, spirit?" asked Marnie.

"Not safe," replied the board.

"Who are you?"

The planchette moved to 'Goodbye'.

"Are you still there?" asked Marnie.

Nothing. Simon tried to stifle the shudder itching to erupt down his back.

"Who was that?" asked Marnie.

"I have no idea, dear, but I don't like that. Why isn't it safe?"

Marnie sat on the floor and stared at the planchette for several moments, but all signs of life had left the board. Simon jammed his hands in his pockets and paced beside the bench.

"Why would an Egyptian princess speak English?"

"Was that her, do you think?"

"Who else could it be?"

Before Simon could answer, the planchette flew off the board, skittering across the floor and bouncing off the platform to land in between the rails. Marnie pushed herself away from the bench. Simon rushed to her side and put his arm around her shoulders as the lights snapped off.

"Simon! What's going on?" Marnie's shoulders trembled.

"I don't know. Never mind though, love. Maybe they just forgot I was here, and they've turned the lights off for the night."

Simon tried to sound sure, but his words sounded hollow. He looked around but he couldn't tell if his eyes were open or closed. The torches were in Marnie's bag, but where was that? Was it near the bench?

A rumble moved towards them in the dark, and Marnie squealed. It sounded like an approaching tube train, but no welcome light rolled into the station. Simon expected the rush of air that accompanied a train, but there was no sudden gust—only a disgusting smell, as though someone had dumped a pile of rotting meat on the platform.

"Oh what is that smell? It's appalling!"

Simon tried hard to breathe through his mouth, fingers pinching his nose. "I don't know. I don't know what's happening." At least the nasal twang of his clamped nose hid the fear in his voice.

"I'm scared, Simon."

"It's okay. I'm here." Simon gave Marnie a squeeze, projecting a bravery that he didn't feel. He clutched her shoulder to stop his hand from shaking.

The rumble stopped, and the smell grew stronger. Something growled in the darkness, and a warm breath rolled across their faces. Beads of sweat stood out on Simon's forehead, sending trickles of liquid terror into his eyes.

"I say there, this is in poor taste! If you mean to frighten us so we lose the bet, then that's a rotten thing to do!" Simon's voice wavered as he called into the shadows.

Nothing replied.

"Where's your bag?" Simon hissed into Marnie's ear.

"By the bench."

Marnie scrabbled across to the bench, and

dumped the contents of her bag onto the platform. The metallic clink of torches hitting tiles sounded louder than thunder in the silence. A torch was pushed into his hand.

Simon fumbled with the switch, but the torch was knocked out of his hand. Warm breath blew in his face, and he fought the urge to gag against the stench of death and decay. A claw raked across one cheek, and he yelped. Something warm and wet dripped down his face—blood. Marnie screamed, and Simon lashed out with one arm. The back of his hand connected with something solid. Were those...scales?

The thing moved. Simon fell forward and landed on his chest. One outstretched arm collided with the missing torch. He snatched it up, pushed himself onto his side then pressed the switch so that a cone of white light tore open the darkness. His mind refused to recognise the hulking beast before him, all sharp angles and wicked teeth. Yellow eyes burned in the torchlight, something approaching malicious intelligence in the depths of its gaze.

A primal instinct, once locked away in the depths of his mind, kicked his fear aside and spurred him to his feet. He brandished the torch as if it were a broadsword. "Get away!"

Baring its teeth, the beast lunged. Without thinking, Simon pushed himself forward and thrust the torch at the creature. It connected with a dull thud, the light sputtering as the creature recoiled. Marnie screamed again as the platform plunged into darkness once more. Simon smacked the torch with his hand and flicked the switch back and forth, but the torch was dead.

"Where's your torch, Marnie?"

"It won't switch on."

Claws sank into Simon's leg and he cried out, the pain blossoming upward towards his hip as blood seeped into the fabric of his trousers. The creature tried to pull him towards it, but a thud sounded in the darkness. The beast's grip relaxed, and Simon scooted backwards towards the wall.

"Marnie?"

"I'm here."

More thuds filled the air, accompanied by screeches that grew more pained. Simon's searching fingers found Marnie and he pulled her close. She clung to him, and they listened to the sounds of a scuffle down the platform. An unearthly wail, part war cry and part death song, echoed throughout the station. Simon remembered the stories of screams heard all the way along at Holborn.

Liquid spattered Simon's face, and he ran his fingers across the viscous mess that wasn't his own blood. That was something else. A final, meaty thud, followed by the sound of something wet being torn apart, punctuated the scuffle. Simon held his breath in the silence.

"Is it over?" asked Marnie after a few moments.

The station lights flickered as they came back on. A heap of scaly flesh lay further down the platform; were it not for the claws on the limb that had been torn off, Simon might not have recognised it for the creature he'd seen in the torchlight. Black blood, thick as tar, covered the tiled floor and dripped over the edge of the platform. A figure stood beside the remains, the adverts on the wall now visible through her fading form. The smell of lotus blossoms masked the stench of gore.

"You're...her, aren't you?" asked Marnie, her eyes wide as she stared at the figure's elaborate headdress.

The figure nodded.

"What is that?"

The planchette reappeared on the board beside Simon, and skated from letter to letter. He read the message to Marnie.

"There are things in the tunnels that should not be woken."

"Did we wake it up?" asked Marnie.

The figure nodded again.

"Is that why you said we weren't safe?" asked Simon.

The figure faded from view but the lotus blossom lingered in the air.

"Thank you, princess," said Marnie.

"Be safe," replied the board.

"Where will you go now?" asked Simon.

"Sleep again." The planchette moved to 'Goodbye'.

The lights grew stronger until steam rose from the remains, and the couple watched the heap of flesh disintegrate into dust. A gust of wind rushed along the platform, taking the dust into the tunnels. Simon looked down, expecting see a gory wound on his thigh.

"My leg!" He pointed at the torn, bloody fabric, and the untouched skin beneath. Marnie poked her fingers through the holes in his trousers, brushing his leg. A shiver ran through Simon, and he wasn't sure if it was Marnie's touch, or the sudden absence of pain.

"Did she heal it?"

"She must have done." Simon guided Marnie's hands away from the blood-soaked rips, and pulled her into a hug.

"What do we do now?" asked Marnie, her words muffled by his jacket.

"We'll put that board away, for one thing."

Marnie wriggled out of his grasp to pack the board and planchette back into her bag. Then she sat on the edge of the bench, looking less wilful than earlier. "Should we admit defeat?"

A waft of lotus blossom drifted past them. Simon smiled. "I don't reckon anything else is going to bother us, do you? Plus it's two AM now, only four more hours to go. Fancy winning thirty pounds?"

Marnie grinned. He sat on the bench and put his arm around her. She snuggled closer, and was soon snoring softly. Simon whispered another thank you to their spectral protector. Despite his bravado, he kept his eyes fixed firmly on the mouth of the tunnel. He couldn't always rely on help, and he wanted to be ready. Simon never wanted to be blasé about the dangers in the darkness again.

Something Wicked This Way Slithered

Something slithers in Cransland House...

S   The words oozed through Lily's mind as she stood under the house's decrepit porch. Water dripped through a hole in the tiles, splashing into a dish grown green with moss beside the door. She looked around to see who had spoken, wondering if her great aunt had employed a gardener or a servant since her last visit. The wide gravelled drive was empty, and no one lurked in the vast laurel hedges that pressed up against the wall.

Lily's finger hovered over the doorbell and she wondered how long she should wait until she rang it again. Aunt Euphemia was pushing seventy, and Lily didn't know what her hearing was like.

Before Lily could push the bell again, a thud sounded from inside the house, and the front door creaked open. Aunt Euphemia stood in the hallway, framed by the gloom beyond. She seemed taller than the last time Lily had seen her, somehow straighter. Her face looked fuller, and fewer wrinkles clustered around her eyes. She'd swapped her pastel twinsets for tweeds, replacing her floral brooch with a circular enamelled pin that depicted a snake eating its own tail.

"Ah, Lily my dear! You made it all right, I see! Did you enjoy the walk from the station?"

Aunt Euphemia held the door open, gesturing for Lily to enter.

Lily stepped across the threshold. The air inside the house felt damp against her skin, and a musty smell hung heavy around her. She fought the urge to shudder. The skylight in the ceiling above the entrance wall was thick with cobwebs, which turned the light grey. Lily had never liked the old relic of a house but it somehow seemed more oppressive, and more funereal than she remembered. Still, with bombs being dropped on London and no end to the war in sight, her mother had thought Lily would have a better time of things in the middle of nowhere.

"I got a lift."

"A lift? From who?"

"Squire Parsons. I think that's what he called himself." Lily shrugged out of her wet mackintosh and hung it on the coat stand by the door. Aunt Euphemia wheeled the ancient metal trolley holding Lily's trunk around and propped it against the wall.

"Ah, Mr Parsons. He's the only one around here that calls himself 'squire'."

Aunt Euphemia pursed her lips, turned on her heel, and marched away down the corridor. Lily frowned. A year ago, her great aunt had shuffled down that passage. When had she become strong enough to march?

Faded old prints and cracked oil paintings of people Lily didn't know lined the corridor. She hurried past them, eager to get to the room at the end. The parlour was always full of light, and Aunt Euphemia often had a blazing fire going in the hearth. Maybe one of her six cats would be dozing in the armchair.

Lily entered the parlour. Moth-eaten net curtains hung at the windows, diffusing the light into a mid-afternoon murk. The tick of the grandfather clock and the downpour outside sounded dead, as though muffled by the sepulchral atmosphere. The furniture looked the same, battered and worn, but a new addition to the room made her pause. A tall glass case stood by the window, and Lily gasped to see a person inside it. Linen grown yellow with age wrapped the figure's limbs, and glimpses of dark skin showed through where the wrappings had worn thin.

"Ah, you've noticed my new acquisition." Aunt Euphemia took up a seat beside the cold fireplace, and gestured that Lily sit on the threadbare sofa opposite. A plate of bread rolls sat on a small table between the seats.

"What is it?" asked Lily. Her stomach roiled, but she couldn't tear her gaze from the case.

"Sit yourself down, Lily, and help yourself to a roll. You must be famished."

Lily picked up a roll from the table and sat.

"That's Merrit-en-Kepi. She's over three thousand years old, and still perfectly preserved."

"Where did you get her?" Lily sniffed at the bread but the sight of the mummy robbed her of her appetite.

"A chap at the local history society came across her and needed somewhere to store her before she went to London. He dropped her off six months ago and never came back for her," replied Aunt Euphemia.

"Doesn't it bother you having a dead body in the house?"

"Not in the slightest. She's long since departed. I think of the mummy as being like an empty house."

But empty houses find occupants, and they aren't always good tenants.

The words drifted through Lily's mind, spoken by the same voice as the one she had heard outside. She looked at Aunt Euphemia but she was partway through demolishing one of the rolls.

"Do you like living here?" asked Lily.

Aunt Euphemia swallowed the last of her bread and nodded.

"It's quiet, probably too quiet for a youngster like yourself, but you get to my age and you just want life to pass you by. How old are you now?"

"Fourteen."

"Ah, I can't even remember being fourteen. Oh! You must be thirsty. I shall just go and fetch the tea."

Aunt Euphemia left the room, leaving a trail of perfume in her wake. Lily screwed up her nose—the scent reminded her of the room at the crematorium where they left a bouquet for her grandfather every year. The floral offerings would rot and give off the same dead plant smell currently following her great aunt around the house.

The dead attract the dead...

Lily started, and looked around the room. Again she saw no sign of the phantom speaker, or any other signs of life. She hadn't seen any of Aunt Euphemia's cats since she'd arrived.

She stood, careful to brush the crumbs onto her plate, and crossed the room to the mummy in the case. Lily laid her fingers on the glass, and yelped. The glass was warm to the touch—warmer than any glass in the dreary parlour had any right to be.

"Careful with her, she's not a toy."

Aunt Euphemia entered the room carrying a tray. Steam curled out of the spout of the pot, and the comforting smell of tea soothed Lily's nerves. She sat back down on the sofa.

"Have you ever opened the case?"

"No. She needs to stay in there. The case must never be opened. Do you understand?"

Lily nodded, stung by her great aunt's sharp tone. Aunt Euphemia's disapproving expression melted as she poured out the tea. Lily wrapped her fingers around her cup and sat back in her seat, happy to oblige when Aunt Euphemia asked for news of London.

* * *

That evening, Lily lay in bed. Aunt Euphemia had let her browse the small library downstairs, and she'd decided to try reading some MR James. Ghost stories seemed the ideal choice for bedtime in such a creaky, murky old house.

Lily's room seemed untouched by the grey damp that pervaded the rest of the house. The walls were cheerful and yellow, and thick rugs covered the floor. A small fire in the hearth crackled behind a screen, and a radio sat on the dresser. Lying in bed with her book, listening to the perpetual rain outside, Lily felt almost at home.

Something slithers in Cransland House...

The voice intruded on Lily's thoughts. She pulled the bedclothes tight around herself, and peered into the flickering shadows cast by her weak lamp.

The dead do not rest easy...

"Wh-who's there?" Lily forced herself to speak out.

Your aunt is in grave danger. You want to help her, don't you?

"Who are you?"

The voice fell silent. Lily frowned. Summoning courage she didn't know she had, she threw back the bedclothes and placed her book on the nightstand.

She explored her room, checking under her bed and inside the wardrobe, but she found no hidden speaker.

Come to the parlour...

Lily spun around when the voice spoke again, aware that it came from nowhere and everywhere at once. It sounded dry, as though dust clogged the throat of the speaker. Dry, and warm. Warm...

Lily thought of the warm glass of the display case and shook her head. The mummy was just a dead body, nothing but a wrapped shell for over three thousand years. She couldn't possibly be the speaker.

You're getting warm...

"Stop talking to me."

Listen to what I must say, and help me, and I shall have no need to talk again...

Lily grunted and crossed the room. She winced as her bare feet met the cold floorboards of the upstairs passage, and she felt her way downstairs through a thick, syrupy darkness. She tried to convince herself that the dull roar of the rain was actually the familiar noise of London, but that moment, she knew she could not be further from home.

After several stumbles and bumped limbs, Lily made it to the downstairs hall. She paused outside the door to the parlour, but the house remained quiet. Aunt Euphemia must be asleep.

Lily turned the handle of the door and slipped into the parlour. The curtains stood open, the weak moonlight diluted by the nets at the window. On impulse, Lily darted across the room and snatched up the poker hanging beside the fireplace.

"Who's there?"

You know who I am.

"Who's talking? Where are you? Show yourself."

You are looking at me.

Her gaze fell upon the display case. The mummy remained in its usual pose, and Lily's defensive stance melted. She let the poker dangle by her side and shook her head to dislodge the strange notion that had made her leave her bed.

"It's all right, I'm just hearing things. There's no one here." Her voice wavered but Lily stood firm.

Of course I am here. I have wanted to help your aunt since I arrived, but no one would hear me. I am glad that you can.

"But you're dead." Lily stared at the display case.

My body is dead but my ka lives on, trapped inside this mortal shell.

"How can you speak English?"

I have been aware of others since my tomb was ransacked. I learned it through listening.

Lily snorted and returned the poker to its hook beside the fireplace.

Do not scoff, young one. I am dead, this is true, but so is your great aunt.

"No she isn't. She looks better than she ever did."

She died shortly after I came here, but her body did not rest. I was not the only relic to be placed in her care, and her death awoke an ancient evil among the amulets.

"I don't believe you."

Open the drawer beneath my feet. You will find a box inside. Open it.

Lily looked down and saw a long, thin handle at the bottom of the case. She knelt on the floor and pulled the handle. A shallow drawer slid forward. A box covered in black leather lay inside. Lily lifted it out and popped the rusty catches on the lid.

Look at what it contains.

An array of pendants and bracelets nestled against velvet padding. Some of them were broken, or had gems missing. Lily ignored them, instead examining the space in the middle of the box. The indentation betrayed the former presence of a circular brooch.

Does it look familiar?

"It looks like Aunt Euphemia's brooch. The snake one."

Something slithers in Cransland House...

"But what does this mean?"

The spirit attached to that brooch now resides within your aunt.

"Nonsense."

It is the truth. It seems docile, for now, but it will not be content with such an existence for long. It will seek to enact destruction, and it will do so using your aunt.

Footsteps on the stairs interrupted the conversation. Lily shoved the box back in the drawer and slid it closed before she jumped up. The door opened. Aunt Euphemia stood framed by the gloom beyond, her white hair pinned up for bed. The snake brooch held her shawl closed.

"What are you doing out of bed?"

"I thought I heard a noise, so I came to check what it was."

"You should have fetched me." Aunt Euphemia's voice skated along a sharp blade, the tone quite unlike the Aunt Euphemia Lily remembered.

"I didn't want to disturb you."

"And yet you have. Go on then, back to bed. I don't want to see you again until the morning."

Lily hung her head and trudged past Aunt Euphemia into the dark hallway beyond. Aunt Euphemia watched her go, and Lily felt disapproving eyes on her until she reached the second floor and the safety of her bedroom.

She climbed back into bed, grateful for the warmth from the dying embers in the hearth, and closed her eyes. Sleep took her hand and led her towards the land of dreams, until a sound jolted Lily awake.

Something hissed in the darkness beyond her door.

* * *

Lily washed and dressed before going downstairs for breakfast. The dark circles under her eyes and her perpetual yawn betrayed her difficult night of sleep, and she hoped Aunt Euphemia wouldn't mention the midnight sojourn to the parlour. The mysterious voice had fallen silent, though Lily expected Aunt Euphemia would find her chores to do that would keep her out of the parlour.

A note on the kitchen table told her that her aunt had gone into the village, and would probably be back by lunchtime. She was instructed to help herself to breakfast, and would she be able to rake up the leaves from the driveway in front of the house? Lily read the note several times, but there was no sign of Aunt Euphemia's anger from the night before.

Lily went outside and fetched the rake from the small outhouse that leaned against the kitchen wall. She found one of Aunt Euphemia's cats, cowering at the rear of the shack behind a hoe. The little tortoiseshell inched forward to sniff Lily's outstretched hand.

"Hello, Pansy. Why are you hiding in here? Why aren't you inside?"

The cat wriggled out from behind the tools and allowed Lily to scratch her behind the ears. Her tiny frame, grown thin from hunger, shuddered as she purred. Lily looked around but saw none of the other cats.

"Aw, poor little Pansy. Why don't you come inside with me?"

Pansy rubbed her head against Lily's hand for a moment. Before Lily could pick up the small cat, Pansy caught sight of something behind Lily, hissed and disappeared back into her hiding place in the outhouse. A shadow fell across the ground, darkening the inside of the lean-to, and all Lily could see was a pair of golden eyes behind the gardening equipment.

"Bloody cats!"

Lily stumbled forward at the sudden roar. The voice sounded both familiar and alien at the same time, and she fell in her hurry to turn around. Something whistled through the air behind Lily's head and landed on the gravel beside her. She recognised it as the rake she'd propped up against the outhouse. Lily forced herself to her feet and turned to face Aunt Euphemia, her eyes burning with an inhuman rage and her smile contorted into a grimace.

"I thought you'd gone into the village!" said Lily, wanting to believe Aunt Euphemia was somehow playing a practical joke.

"I've been! But look at how long it's taken you to get your lazy behind out of bed—and you've been wasting time with that stupid animal instead of doing your chores!" Aunt Euphemia lunged past Lily and snatched up the rake once more.

Lily scrabbled backwards and ducked as her aunt took another swing. The metal spikes nicked her face, and the momentum sent her sprawling onto her back. Lily caught sight of Pansy disappearing further into the outhouse as she struggled to her feet.

Aunt Euphemia whirled the rake backwards for another swing, and Lily seized her chance. She darted forward, knocked Aunt Euphemia off her feet, and raced for the front door. It stood ajar, the way she'd left it, and she thumped it open with the palms of her hands.

Lily! Lily! Come to me!

Lily ran towards the voice and burst into the parlour. She turned the key in the lock and backed away into the room. Scratchings and scrapings in the hall gave way to a pummelling on the door. Lily looked around for a weapon but the poker and battered old toasting fork no longer rested by the fireplace.

Only I can end this. Open my case.

Lily stared at the parlour door, rattling in its frame with each attack. She couldn't fight off the thing that used to be her aunt; she'd only managed to barely escape as it was. Lily turned and fiddled with the catch holding the case closed. She threw open the door, but the mummy just stood there.

"What are you waiting for?"

You must restore life to me. Place your hands on my head.

Lily grimaced, but laid a hand on each side of the mummy's head. Protective tar coated the skin in place of its wrappings, and it left the face feeling smooth but cold. Lily tried hard not to think that this had once been a living person with her own hopes and dreams.

Now tell me you give me life.

Lily hesitated for a moment, until another crash at the door made her jump.

"I give you life! I give you life!"

A peal of laughter echoed inside Lily's head, morphing into a harsh banshee cackle. She tore her hands away from the mummy, clamping them over her ears as she dropped to her knees. She pressed her hands harder against her skull but the cackle grew louder. The hinges of the parlour door screamed as a final crack to the door broke the lock. Lily squeezed her eyes shut and waited for the blow.

* * *

Consciousness returned with the sounds of scuffling. Lily tried to force her eyes open, but her eyelids wouldn't cooperate. She remembered clamping her hands over her ears, and she tried to move them to better hear the fight in the parlour. Her hands were no longer over her ears, but rather bound to her sides. She tried to flex her fingers but there was no movement.

A grey light erupted at the edges of her awareness, and the room swam into view, emerging in a blurred haze as though appearing through fog. Aunt Euphemia grappled with a shorter figure, her fingers contorted into claws that dug into the young girl's shoulders. For her part, the girl had her hands wrapped around Aunt Euphemia's throat. Lily recognised the blond braid swinging down the girl's back. It was her braid.

The Not-Lily squeezed tighter, and Aunt Euphemia's grip loosened. She released her hold of the girl's shoulders and clawed at the hands around her throat. Lily tried to scream but her mouth wouldn't move, and no sound came out. Her heart would not even beat harder, nor would her stomach churn. The Not-Lily forced Aunt Euphemia onto the floor, and tore the snake brooch from her cardigan. She dropped it onto the exposed boards and crushed it beneath her foot. The old woman turned slack, the fight evaporating from her hands. Her eyes rolled back in her head, and her jaw dropped open. Lily fought to make her lips move, to form words she might hurl at the imposter, but she was held rigid, trapped inside a body that didn't obey her.

The Not-Lily turned and pranced across the parlour towards her. Up close, Lily could see the imposter was her mirror image in every way, except her eyes were brown, instead of Lily's usual grey.

"You see? I kept my promise. I defeated her." The imposter spoke with Lily's voice, but its tones sounded alien to her ears. She wasn't used to hearing herself outside of her own head.

What's wrong with me? Why can't I move? Lily couldn't speak but she could still think.

"You granted me life, Lily. In particular, you granted me *your* life. I am most grateful."

Lily screamed, and the Not-Lily chuckled. The imposter closed the glass door to the case, and fastened the catch. Lily hurled obscenities learned from her bricklayer uncle, but the imposter ignored her. She swept the shards of the brooch into the dustpan from the fireplace, and tipped them onto a newspaper that she folded into an envelope. The Not-Lily left the parlour, dragging Aunt Euphemia's body behind her. Moments later, Lily listened as the imposter called her mother to inform her of her aunt's tragic end.

Two days later, Lily heard a car pull up outside the house. She hadn't seen the imposter since the day of the body swap, and the Not-Lily had ignored all of her pleas and threats. Back in a body after so many centuries, Merrit-en-Kepi was in no hurry to give it up again.

The front door slammed, followed by a car door. As the engine note faded away to nothing, Lily cried her consciousness to sleep.

The Cursed One

The girl sits in a chair by the window, the moonlight cascading through the glass to cast half her face in shadow. She hums as she rocks from side to side, her eyes closed. I still do not believe she can lead us to Seven, yet Edward claims she is highly recommended by the Order. She looks more like a street urchin than a psychic, yet we need her guidance if we are to locate the creature in time.

To my right, Robert senses my discomfort, and draws me to one side. 'What ails you, Henry?'

'I remain unconvinced.' Robert knows to what I allude, since I voiced my doubts at length before she arrived, to varied protestations from Edward.

'We need her.'

'I agree that we need a guide. I am just unsure that she is the one we need.' I gesture to the girl, who now draws symbols in the air before her.

Edward stares at her, enraptured. This is indeed a strange reversal in our roles, for it is usually I who am accused of being too trusting, or even gullible. Edward is normally our indefatigable leader.

The girl cries out and sits bolt upright in her chair. She grips the arm rests and strains forward, as though restricted by a force we cannot see.

'I see it!' she hisses through her yellow teeth.

'What do you see?' Edward snatches up the parchment and pen beside him, ready to take notes.

'A quiet canal, away from the noise of the Carnevale. The windows...they are all shuttered. No one can see. The water...it ripples. It boils, as though it lives.'

I cannot imagine a single part of Venice being quiet during the Carnevale, but I keep my snort of derision to myself. If she is right, then this may give us some insight as to where Seven might leave the water.

'The water parts. Something climbs out. It is tall, with a long snout, and it is covered in scales. It shakes itself dry as a dog might.'

Edward scribbles the descriptions, but it is no use. Seven does not keep its natural form on land – he knows that as well as I, if not better. It was upon his insistence that I applied to join the Order, and he knew about the initiation long before he saw fit to tell me about it. We have been charged to journey to the watery city to track down and capture Seven, one of the Cursed Ones. If we are successful, we may join the Order. This is the first time that the initiation has included the loathsome creature that dwells in the canals.

'It is changing. It has chosen a new face. I see it shedding scales, becoming smaller, more delicate.'

'What form has it assumed?' asks Edward.

'It is a young woman, naked as a babe. She has hair like burnished copper, and skin like fresh cream. Oh, she is so beautiful.'

Now that is a useful insight. According to the folio, locals believe it to be bad luck to gaze into the water at midnight, but they cannot know how right they are, for Seven steals the reflections of those who do, and chooses a new form each year chosen from among these faces. Somewhere in the world, a young woman with copper hair who once visited Venice and admired her features in the moonlit canal has dropped dead as Number Seven assumed her form. She will not have stood a chance.

'She has found a house with loose shutters, and has made her way inside. She seeks clothes. Oh! Oh! I am lost! She has seen me!'

The psychic thrashes in her chair, and Edward reaches out to steady her. She throws off his reassuring touch, and clamps her hands over her ears, kicking at the floor, her mouth foaming like that of a rabid dog. Robert and I rush forward but we cannot get past her flailing arms and legs. A particularly vicious kick sends Robert flying backward. I reach for her but my fingers grasp only fabric as she judders out of the chair. She goes limp as she falls to the floor, blood dribbling from her nose.

'Seven killed her. It did so without even being here.' Edward stares at the dead psychic.

'And it will do the same to us if we linger here. We must find it and capture it.' Robert rubs his hip as he clambers to his feet.

Edward gathers his notes, and he leaves a message for Basil, our contact within the Order. Someone will need to tidy away the girl.

* * *

We decide that the best way to locate Seven is to split up. Venice is a labyrinth of squares and alleyways, although we know from our intelligence that the creature will make for a crowded place to begin hunting. It will seek an older gentleman, wise in the ways of the world and yet not so old as to be descending into infirmity. I understand now why it has chosen this particular form. Its prey will be flattered by the attentions of a beautiful young woman, and flattery leads to trust.

We each don a mask, and head our separate ways. Robert will begin with the Campo San Moise, and Edward will survey the Campo San Maurizio. I am to check the Campo Sant'Angelo before we converge upon the Campo Santo Stefano. If we are not successful, we can exclude the western tip of San Marco from our search.

The squares are busy, filled with bustling crowds who have yet to make their way to the main festivities of the Piazza San Marco. Harlequins rub shoulders with plague doctors as people seek to enjoy the music that fills the air. Dancing and revelry surrounds me, and a faint tinge of panic colours my thoughts. I understand why the Order has chosen Seven as their prey, but I do not understand why they have turned its capture into an initiation rite. Previous applicants have stalked vampires, or fished for mermaids – they have not sought the Cursed Ones.

I memorised the contents of the folio before I left London, and I allow my thoughts to wander as I pick my way between dancing couples and tumbling jesters. Seven is the youngest of the Cursed Ones, those ancient creatures who dwell in the dark, deep places of the world. Their names cannot be pronounced by human mouths, though civilisations throughout the centuries have given them titles befitting their status. Seven has also been called La Musicale Morte – the Musical Death.

The music of Antonio Vivaldi fills the square, and the people cheer Venice's favourite son, though he has been dead some twenty years. I curse the musicians with their proficient playing, as it distracts me from my purpose. According to the folio, the surest way to recognise Seven is the music it sings in the mind when it is close at hand. I hear nothing but the strains of the Winter concerto, and I am torn between relief and concern. I have read of the Musical Death's exploits, and its flair for the dramatic when displaying its kills, though such reports never make their way into the newspapers.

I make several circuits of the square, nodding to other English gentlemen whom I vaguely recognise from London society, but those enjoying the revelry are basking in the flush of youth. They are not at all to Seven's taste. It will seek an older gentleman, brimming with experience, and most likely in Venice to drown his sorrows after a failed love affair. The Order sent very specific notes on this particular point. Not for the first time I find myself wondering why such an elusive creature has become the focus of their initiation – if the finest agents have been unable to capture Seven, then why should I, or Robert, or Edward, fare better?

My ruminations continue as I stroll across the square and make my way along the Calle Frati Dorsoduro towards the Campo Santo Stefano. The narrow street curves between the tall buildings, and the rooftops blot out the night sky. The windows are shuttered for the night, and no candlelight spills into the Calle. I run a hand along the building to my left, keeping my eyes focused on the blaze of light in the square beyond. My ears prick at the slightest sound, attuned to the back alleys of London where a search for a werewolf might also lead to an encounter with a thief, and my heart pounds until I reach the relative safety of the square.

More festivities swirl around me as I join the crowd. I wave to Lord Tilmore as he saunters past. He wears a plain black domino mask, but I recognise the giant auburn beard that covers the lower half of his face. The buttons of his coat strain as the fabric swells over the bulge of his stomach. We often speak when we meet in London. I have always found Lord Tilmore to be a genial fellow, quick of wit and the owner of a booming laugh that can be heard throughout Mayfair, though he has been more melancholy of late after the death of his wife.

The plan blooms in my mind in an instant. Lord Tilmore is the exact sort of man Seven will favour. Full of life, though sad, and only just shy of fifty. His force of personality will sustain Seven's psychic abilities, while the meat of his ample figure will provide sustenance until the Carnevale next year, when it will next be able to adopt human form. The melancholy no doubt adds some sort of flavour to the flesh that I am unable to fathom.

Venice may yet be filled with men who equally suit Seven's tastes, but I follow Lord Tilmore at a respectful distance. He is perhaps my best chance of luring Seven into the open, and there I shall try to divert it from completing its feast. I can rescue my friend and capture my objective at the same time.

Lord Tilmore makes a circuit of the square, and I hang back, unwilling to jeopardise the chance of Seven making contact if Lord Tilmore appears to be accompanied. My heart hammers, and I force myself to calm my ragged nerves, lest the creature hears the pounding in my chest. Young women dance around me, giggling and clutching at my hands. A primal part of myself wishes to dance with them, to enjoy the festivities and pursue the sorts of liaisons that beget scandals in London, but a life hangs in the balance. I disentangle myself from their advances, returning their pretty smiles but retaining Lord Tilmore in the corner of my eye.

Lord Tilmore heads for the narrow opening that is the Calle dello Spezier. It leads to the Campo San Maurizio, and I decide to follow in the hope that Edward is still there. I can tell him my plan, and we can send word to Robert. A throng swarms down the street in the same direction, and I allow the crowd to carry me along. We cross the Rio del Santissimo over a small bridge, and the Calle takes us into the square. A fiddler stands at the doorway to the church, and dancers whirl in a frenzy before him. Lord Tilmore makes for a palazzo across the Campo.

I cannot see Edward, but he is not my concern. I watch as a young lady sashays across the square and wraps her long white fingers around Lord Tilmore's arm. They exchange a few words that I cannot hear, stolen as they are by the music around me, but Lord Tilmore throws his head back, the movements of his belly betraying his laugh. A cold fist of fear grips my stomach when I realize the young lady has hair like burnished copper.

All attempts at subtlety are cast aside, and I push through the crowd towards them. A tall man in a bauta mask blocks my path, and black eyes glare down at me. I mumble an apology but once I have squeezed past him, Lord Tilmore is gone. I am only in time to see the door to the palazzo swing closed.

'Henry!'

A clear voice cuts through the laughter and music of the square, and I turn to see Edward forcing his way between a group of giggling young women.

'Edward! I have seen it, I have seen Seven!'

'I wondered why you were here. I thought we were meeting in Santo Stefano.'

'It's gone after Lord Tilmore!'

Edward gasps and turns toward the palazzo. Together we make our way through the throng and slip inside. The usual valet is occupied with a tall woman in a plain white mask, and we creep up the stairs to our right.

The strains of a violin drift through my mind, not heard as one might hear an orchestra or a musician performing nearby, but heard solely inside my head. The effect throws me off balance and I almost fall, gripping the bannister to keep me upright. Edward clutches the bannister on the other side of the staircase, one hand pressed to the side of his head.

'It is La Musicale Morte,' he whispers.

I nod, and I force myself onward. The music is not unpleasant, more melancholy, but the sensation of hearing music not made by physical instruments creates an unbearable dizziness. Every time I place my foot on the next step, a wave of nausea sends me reeling. We have not the time for this, and we battle onward, as though held back by an invisible tide.

The music grows to a roar as we reach the second floor, and we fight to reach the suite of rooms on the right hand side of the corridor. Inside, Lord Tilmore sprawls on the floor, pressing himself against the wall as though he might dissolve through it and escape his captor. His eyes are glazed with fear, his lips muttering the word 'no' over and over again.

Seven stands over him, the beautiful young woman now a discarded skin on the floor. Black scales cover its hide, and its talons reflect the light like mother-of-pearl daggers. It swings its head towards us, its long jaws open to reveal a mouth full of jagged teeth. Terror paralyses me – I expected it to retain its form before it made its kill so as to preserve the victim. I didn't expect to see La Musicale Morte in all its hideous glory.

Edward tries to intervene but his words are lost in a strangled cry that dies in his throat. He is as stricken as I am, and neither of us knows what to do next. The Order did not prepare us for this moment. We are not armed, since Robert has our weapons – we thought we would make the capture together. He is the one who knows where to take Seven, yet we do not, even if we managed to overwhelm a creature more ancient than fear itself. For a second, I feel like a sacrificial lamb, sent to the slaughterhouse on behalf of the Order.

Shouts are heard in the stairwell, and Seven pauses, its gaze fixed on the open doorway behind us. Its eyes are peculiar, I expected them to be yellow, or red, like the demons of the childhood tales I grew up with. Yet they are pale green, spangled with stars, and filled with a mixture of desperation and sorrow.

Four men burst into the room. Three of them bear flintlocks, while one of them carries a violin. All are dressed in the stark black frock coats of the Order of the Sphinx, and wear plain black masks. The violinist takes up his instrument and begins a mournful melody that harmonises with the music in my head. Edward sags beside me, no longer struck down by the awful concerto perpetrated by Seven. The melancholy tune drowns out the psychic music, and my heart slows, returning to something resembling normality.

Yet the tune changes, and the rapid notes neutralize the song of La Musicale Morte altogether. Seven screeches, a sound that cracks the glass in the windows, and drops to its knees. It is still howling and clutching at its head when the three men bearing flintlocks overpower it, and descend upon it with chains.

* * *

The men escort us across the Grand Canal to the narrow waterways of the San Polo district. A jetty takes us to a small, quiet square away from the bustle of the city, and we head inside the church that nestles between two silent buildings. Someone fetched Robert, and he remains at the palazzo with Lord Tilmore, who is traumatised but physically unharmed. So far, it would appear that both of my goals have been met.

The men drag Seven into the church, the violinist never faltering in his music. Every few steps one of the men kicks the creature, and it gives up attempting to defend itself. I wince with every blow that lands on the beast, and Edward and I follow them into the cool, dusty darkness. Hundreds of candles cast their soft glow, though the flickering light turns the cherubs into demons, and the saints into sinners.

Nine men wearing black robes stand in front of the altar, and I recognize the Earl of Cragmore in the centre. I should have known that the Inquisitor of the Order would be present. Seven is deposited in front of him, where it curls into a ball at his feet. The violinist continues to play his music of subjection, accompanied by the creature's whimpers, and a pang of pity tugs at my heart. How can it be that this Cursed One, this ancient being, is reduced to such a state by a mere rhapsody?

'Gentlemen, you've done well,' says the Earl.

'Well, I rather think these fellows did the hard work,' says Edward, gesturing to our black-clad companions.

'Nonetheless, it was you that led them to the creature in the first place. You have passed the initiation.'

Edward smiles, relief burned into his expression, but I find the commendation does not satisfy me in the same way.

'What will you do with it?' The words are out of my mouth before I can stop myself.

'Dare you ask questions of the Inquisitor?' One of the flintlock-wielding men steps forward, brandishing his pistol at me.

'It's alright, Rutherford. Step down. These young men have encountered something extraordinary; it is only natural they will have questions.'

The man steps back, but he continues to glare at me.

'This is La Musicale Morte, known also as Seven. It is the youngest of the Cursed Ones. But you know this, you've read the folio.'

Edward and I nod. The Earl steps forward and begins to pace, adopting the stance of a professor commencing a great lecture.

'Good. Of course you have. That's how you knew to pick a target to lure it out into the open. That's why you were chosen for this initiation. We knew you would think differently. You would get things done.'

He smiles at us like a benevolent father, but I still

cannot see the sense in his words. The Earl sees our silence as an acceptance of the compliment, and continues.

'Here at the Order, we pride ourselves on ridding the world of unnatural beings, making it a safer place for God's creatures to live.'

A question springs into my mind as I wonder why these unnatural beings are not also considered to be God's creation, but I manage to quiet myself before I can voice my disagreement.

'Imagine if we learned a way of commanding creatures with more power than ourselves. We could rid the world of these beings more quickly, and more safely. Did you know that we lost eighteen members of the Order last year?'

Edward and I shake our heads, although Robert said something to that effect yesterday.

'Werewolves, vampires, sirens, poltergeists – they all need to be dealt with.'

The Earl lashes out with one foot, landing a blow in what I presume is the creature's ribs. It howls, and somewhere in the church a window breaks. It throws back its head to glare at the Earl but its gaze falls upon me. I stare into those eyes, those fathomless eyes that speak of the deep, and the time before time, and something in my mind begins to flex.

'This creature here is the answer. We shall break its will, and bend it to ours. We may use it to command the other Cursed Ones, and use their power to rid the world of the unnatural and the unwanted!'

The Earl looks at the other men, his face shining with fervour and pride, and they nod with enthusiasm. Even Edward gazes at the Earl as a poor man might gaze at a hunk of prime beef, and sickness unravels in my stomach. This is wrong. What right have we to determine the fate of a creature so much older than ourselves? What right has the Earl to wield its power in place of his own?

Before I can realize what I intend to do, the flexing thing in my mind snaps, and I rush forwards to seize the violin. I snatch up the bow and hurl it across the church where it snaps against a pillar. The other men try to overpower me but I smash the instrument against the pew to my right.

The perverse congregation erupts in confusion. Men try to seize me, and Edward pleads with me, but I think of nothing but the creature on the floor. Only it isn't on the floor, it stands now, its chains lying in broken links at its feet. Music bursts into life in my head, but this is not the confusing concerto from the palazzo, this is a triumphant chorus of justice and power. The men with flintlocks switch their attention from me to Seven, but their shots are useless against its scaly hide. Everyone tries to fight while scrabbling at their ears, yet I cannot understand their pain. Do they not see the joy and glory of this moment?

Seven's talons and teeth flash in the dim light of the church, and I hear the distant sound of bones breaking, and men screaming. Soon the air is filled with the tangy scent of blood, and I slip on the floor as I try to persuade Edward to run. He stares at me with the wild-eyed gaze of a broken man, and Seven lets him go as he bolts from the church, the last survivor of the Order of the Sphinx's Venetian Council.

La Musicale Morte envelops me with music, a comforting symphony of gratitude and grace, and I sense its arms around me as I give in to the music. All of time and space opens itself before me, and my mind breaks apart like cobwebs in the wind as I fall into an abyss of nothingness.

I awake some time later, not as Henry, but as part of something bigger. I am part of La Musicale Morte now, entwined in its music as I lend my voice to its chorus. We leave the church as we are now sated, and we slip back into the water from which we emerged just hours previously.

We are satisfied now, and we will rest. For now.

The Jar by the Door

The old stairs creaked with every step. Joseph grimaced; unable to decide what made more noise – the staircase or his joints.

He cursed the building between each laboured breath. Six floors of crumbling apartments above his own dingy quarters – that was six floors of leaking pipes and irritating tenants, including 5B.

Make that *especially* 5B.

Joseph paused for breath on the landing below the top floor – home to 6B.

The current inhabitant had taken one look at the place seven weeks ago, and declared it perfect for her needs. Her long legs and narrow waist told Joseph she'd be perfect for his needs, but he was old enough to be her grandfather. Not that it had ever stopped him before. Joseph never considered that his wandering hands might be the reason he had such a high turnover of tenants.

He hoped he might catch the leggy blonde stepping out of the shower, just like he had with 2A three weeks ago when he casually dropped around to check the radiators.

Movement scuffled inside 5B, and Joseph snatched at the bannister. Too slow to escape, he stared as the door swung inward and 5B poked her head into the hallway. A silk headscarf covered the rollers in her auburn hair, and she pursed her already-pinched lips.

"Mr Petersen, I thought I heard you."

"Indeed you did. If you'll excuse me though..."

"Are you going upstairs?"

"Well that was my plan but right now I'm standing here talking to you." Joseph couldn't resist the snide comment. She mentioned her 'important work' and bandied around terms like 'research', 'imperative' and 'funding' every time she spoke to him, so insulting her intelligence became a small victory for Joseph.

"He's getting worse." She glared at him but didn't bother to conceal the ice in her tone.

"Who?"

"6B."

"You must be mistaken; a woman lives in 6B."

"I'm never mistaken."

Joseph shrugged and placed one foot on the bottom step. "Well I'm here now, and I've got a list of your complaints, so I'll head up to see what's going on."

"They aren't complaints, Mr Petersen, they're issues. And issues need to be resolved."

Joseph nodded, and turned away. Her glare bored into his back as he mounted the stairs. All thoughts of catching 6B in the shower melted away, replaced by irritation with 5B.

What did she mean, saying a man lived in 6B? There was no way the delectable blonde was a man – and he should know who he rented out his apartments to. True, there was always the chance she was sub-letting – maybe it was a man causing all the problems for 5B, and 6B didn't even know about it.

He nodded, satisfied that his theory allowed 6B to remain unblemished while putting the blame onto a stranger that he could evict.

He reached the top of the stairs, crossed the landing to 6B, and rapped his gnarled knuckles against the flaking wood.

"Miss? Are you in? It's just me, Joseph," he called. Everyone else in the building called him Mr Petersen but she could call him by his first name. He decided that she would appreciate a gesture like that.

He knocked again. No reply. How typical – he'd come all this way for nothing. He glared down the staircase in the vague direction of 5B, aware that her door was still open. The nosy snob complained about everyone in the building, but she had been complaining about 6B more than anyone else for two weeks now.

Suspicious noises, foul smells, dubious visitors – 5B filed a new complaint every day about the same things. Joseph knew he should have ignored her, but he wanted an excuse to ogle 6B's cleavage. Besides, he hadn't been inside the flat since she moved in, and he liked checking on his property from time to time.

Joseph raised his hand to knock again when the first whiff caught in his nostrils. He screwed up his face and bunched his fist up to his nose. Perhaps a rat had died inside the wall cavity. Or maybe he'd stepped in something.

Against his better judgement, he sniffed again, and retched. The stench of rotting meat and rising damp came from beyond the door. Whatever it was needed fixing...which meant he'd need to pay for it.

There again, 6B hadn't informed him of any problems and that worried him, especially in a fleapit like this where something was always going wrong. Maybe she was hurt – something might have happened to her. Or this elusive male tenant might be hurt, and she didn't even know about it.

"Mr Petersen?"

Joseph groaned as 5B came up the stairs. She wore a shapeless green cardigan and a disapproving expression. Joseph guessed she was annoyed at having to abandon her beloved research. Well she didn't need to interrupt writing her book to babysit him.

"Yes?"

The words on 5B's lips died as she reached the smell on the landing. Her face twisted, and her nose screwed up as though it could crawl up her forehead away from the stench.

"What on earth is that smell? Really, these incidents have been getting worse but this really does top them all!"

"I was about to find out what it is when you came upstairs."

Joseph rummaged in the left pocket of his worn corduroy trousers and found a crumpled tissue. He stuffed it up his nose and fished his jangling bunch of keys out of his right pocket.

He fumbled with the correct one, eventually getting the ancient metal bone into the lock. The keyhole protested for a moment, as if aware that it was not 6B entering the apartment, but the door ignored the keyhole's misgivings and eased inward an inch. Joseph gave the door a final hard shove, and stepped inside.

He shuffled down the narrow hallway into the living room. Newspapers covered the windows, with narrow shafts of light penetrating the occasional gap between already-yellow sheets. The sunshine fell across bare floorboards covered in tattered old clothing. Joseph glared at the mess, furious with her lack of housekeeping but blind to the fact the clothes were not the style he'd seen 6B wear.

"Is he home, do you think?" 5B called out from the

doorway, clearly unwilling to step inside. Well, Joseph didn't blame her.

"You can go back downstairs, I can take it from here," he replied.

He listened for a moment but heard no footsteps on the stairs. *The nosy cow isn't leaving until I do.*

The tissue in his nose came loose, and Joseph realised the smell came from the bathroom. He felt his way through the apartment, stumbling over assorted junk and rubbish.

He peered into the gloom and realised that 6B had very little furniture; in fact, there was nothing of her own, simply the battered basics he'd provided. He'd had students like this, who left discarded plates of food dotted about the room, although he couldn't see any leftover meals lying around. If anything, the kitchenette was an oasis of relative calm in the chaos of the apartment.

He groped across the wall and found the light switch. The bathroom light sputtered into life, casting its weak glow into the hallway. Joseph looked down, his gaze caught by something dark and sticky that covered the floorboards in front of the bathroom door. He gagged, and forced himself not to vomit. He pushed the door open with his elbow, desperate not to touch anything with his bare hands. Not even 6B herself.

Mental note, I'll serve her a termination in the morning. Just hope she tidies up before she goes.

Joseph paused in the doorway, jaw slack and eyes bulging, as he saw a sticky, red mess in the bath tub, all sinews and awkward angles. Crimson handprints stained the wash basin. Three suits hung from coat hangers dangling from the shower rail. More bile rushed up Joseph's throat when he realised they weren't suits

They were skins.

He stumbled backwards, willing himself to look away from the skins hung up to dry. He glanced in the mirror and saw rows of jars lined up on the shelves behind the bathroom door. Joseph urged himself not to turn around, but he was facing the other way before he realised he'd moved. A multitude of eyeless faces stared back from inside the jars, floating in dark green liquid.

A scream bubbled up in Joseph's throat, but a pain in his chest swallowed the sound. He dropped to the floor, his knees popping under the strain. One hand clutched at his shirt, twisted into a claw as if he sought to tear open his chest and free his burning heart.

Joseph slumped across the filthy floorboards in the bathroom; too infected by pain to realise there should have been lino on the floor. The agony set his lungs on fire as he struggled to take fitful breaths, torn at the edges and too shallow to be useful.

"Mr Petersen? I heard a thud, are you alright?" 5B's voice drifted along the hallway. He scrabbled towards the door, his fingers raking through the congealed mess on the floor, and he made it across the threshold. He tried to crawl further along the passage towards the front door but his legs refused to obey. Panic gripped him, and he croaked a plea for help. The pain stole his words and his mouth flapped silently as footsteps approached along the hall.

"Oh my God, Mr Petersen!"

His vision darkened, and the floorboards creaked as she knelt beside him. She felt his neck for a pulse, prodding below his ear.

"Stay here, I'll go and phone for an ambulance." She stood and ran out of the door. Joseph grimaced, despite the pain – where did she think he was going to go?

Another fist of agony gripped his heart, and he fought for breath, willing it into his wheezing lungs. He ceased to care whether 5B had found her mobile, and he was no longer interested in serving 6B with a termination notice. When his ribs stopped heaving, he looked for all the world like another pile of old rags.

* * *

Effie Wade, also known among other less flattering things as 5B by her landlord and neighbours, hurried along the hallway towards the safety of the landing.

She'd barely registered the mess in the apartment, but the darkness was difficult to miss. Really, didn't Mr Petersen check the references of his tenants? Her own had been impeccable, of course, although it was a constant source of irritation that she had to live in a place like this to start with. At least once she'd finished her book, then things would be different. They simply had to be.

She was halfway down the stairs, cursing herself for not bringing her mobile phone with her, when she heard footsteps below. Her neighbour in 5A was away for the week, and 6A never returned before 5pm, so it could only be 6B himself. Perhaps he had a mobile phone she could use – it was the least he could do, given it was probably the state of the flat that had given Mr Petersen a heart attack.

Effie reached the bottom of the stairs and waited. Moments later, the short man from 6B appeared on the landing. He stared at her with those cold, dead eyes of his, and she suppressed a shudder.

"I can help you?" The rasp of his voice grated on Effie's already-shattered nerves, and she decided to overlook his poor grasp of English for the time being.

"Do you have a telephone? A mobile phone? Mr Petersen has been taken ill in your flat, I need to phone for an ambulance."

"Telephone is in flat. You come."

The short man slid past her and clumped up the stairs, pausing once to nod his head upwards. Effie grimaced and followed him. *Why didn't I think to look*

for a phone in the flat? I could have called an ambu-
lance and been waiting downstairs by now.

Effie hurried back up the stairs after him, for-
getting about her book for the first time in weeks.
She found the short man from 6B standing outside
his open door, his head tilted back as he sniffed
the air.

"We should be in more of a hurry. Mr Petersen
needs an ambulance now," she said.

"Yes, yes."

6B toddled into the apartment. Effie watched him
disappear into the gloom and thought again about
what an odd gait he had. Perhaps he had some sort
of mobility problems, which could explain the strange
noises at night.

"Ah. Mr Landlord. This is not good." The short
man's voice sounded hollow inside the flat. Effie edged
closer to the door, unwilling to step inside. She held
the sleeve of her cardigan over her mouth in an attempt to blot out the stench.

"He needs an ambulance!" she shouted through
her sleeve. What on earth was he doing?

"You come, sit with him while I call."

Effie groaned, and stepped into the apartment.
She kept her eyes fixed on the dim glow of the bathroom, ignoring the voices in her head that screamed
warnings about heading to the light.

Mr Petersen lay where she'd left him, and her fingers again sought out his pulse. Nothing fluttered
against her fingers; no fragile attempt to cling to life.
Gently she lifted his body to check his face, to maybe close his eyes, but a scream erupted in her throat
when she saw the smear of blood across the front of
his shirt. She followed the trail down his body and
along the floor, leading into the bathroom.

She hauled herself up onto shaking legs, clinging to the door frame for support. She peered into the
bathroom, and another scream, this one too violent

to be born, paralysed her throat as she took in the bloody skins hung up to dry above the bath.

"You should not have come."

Effie whirled around at the sound of 6B's voice, but the bat connected with her skull before she could see he was armed. Stars exploded across her vision, and she screamed at her legs not to fail her. They ignored her, and she crumpled to the floor, one hand landing in the sticky pool beside Mr Petersen. She fell unconscious to the sounds of her own voice berating her for ever getting involved.

* * *

The short man stood over the body of the woman. He recognised her from 5B – she was the creature that filed endless complaints against him. Stupid woman – what business did she have in his den? She would be downstairs in her own little abyss working on more things to complain about if she had just left things alone. Alone...yes, she was lonely. He smelled it on her on the stairs. She reeked of it. So did the landlord. All those pheromones when he wore the blond woman. Disgusting.

The short man sniffed the air to be sure. No, no signs of life here. Recently, yes, but not now. He snapped off the bathroom light, his eyes happiest in the gloom. He liked darkness, a comforting blanket that blotted out the world.

He nudged 5B aside with his foot. The landlord lay prone on the floor, one hand at his chest, his face twisted into an expression that could have been anger or inflamed passion. The short man smirked, thinking of the man's lust. *Heartache after all.*

The short man reached his fingers around the back of his neck and pried the skin away from a glistening black spinal column. The skin peeled away easily, and the creature stepped out of the suit. It unfurled its long limbs and stretched, its joints popping as they snapped back into place. It was glad to be free of the short man's prison, able to move long legs at more than an awkward shuffle. It crossed the corridor to the bedroom and hung the suit in the wardrobe, beside the tall attractive woman's skin. Oh yes, the landlord had liked that skin. He'd made that very clear.

The creature gently peeled away its human face, and deposited it in the empty jar by the door. It took up the skinning knife from the cabinet and skittered back into the corridor where it bent its long nose and sniffed the landlord.

No scent of life, but it didn't hurt to be sure.

It nudged the landlord with one claw. Nothing. The creature allowed itself a tiny crow of satisfaction. Yes, this was very good. The other tenants would let it in now, dressed as their landlord. And two for the price of one. The tenant in 5B would make a lovely new suit. Very roomy.

Light flashed on the creature's blade. It swayed with joy, humming the opening bars to *Eleanor Rigby* as it worked. It didn't understand music, not really, but it understood that humans liked it, and that in itself was useful information. It often found new skins at the discotheque three streets away, where humans copulated in the alleyway and deposited the contents of their stomachs on the pavement. Those skins needed an awful lot of cleaning.

The landlord proved to be especially easy – age had loosened his skin, and the creature hung him up in the bathroom with the others. It had a vague understanding of commerce, and it needed finance to pay its rent. Besides, others would come once the landlord was missed, but it would be gone by then, set up in another building in another town.

There was a much bigger city several miles away that it could try. Perhaps it would even find another of its kind, hiding in plain sight. The creature did not understand loneliness, but it did understand its need to hear the clicks and whistles of its own language, its desire to curl up alongside the insectoid form of another.

It took longer to prepare 5B. The creature berated itself for using the bat, and carefully removed the scalp around the wound. Perhaps it could use the blonde woman's hair instead. No one in the building knew 5B that well. They may not even notice.

The creature could sense that night had fallen by the time it had finished with 5B. Her skin hung alongside the landlord's, her face in a jar by the bathroom door. It left their remains in the bath tub to congeal – raw flesh tasted too metallic for its palate. The creature preferred a flavour of age in its meals.

Thoughts of food turned once again to money. The creature knew it would need more money for a flat somewhere else – and without 5B snooping around, or the landlord getting under its feet, it could find money in the very same building.

Once again the blond woman's skin was selected from the wardrobe, and the creature slipped into its long limbs and tiny waist with ease. It contorted its face to match the contours of the woman, and stretched to allow the skin to settle. This skin would last for some time, its form better suited to the creature than the short man.

It tottered out of the flat on too-high heels. Music came from the flat next door, and the creature peered out of the landing window. A clock hung outside the pawnbroker's across the street, and it announced the time as 7:30pm. 6A was home now – and the creature remembered the way the young man looked at the blond woman. 6A would let it in.

The creature listened, and attempted a smile when it recognised the song coming from inside 6A. *Eleanor Rigby.*

It knocked on the door.

The Charterhouse Bullies

Edward stood in the shadows inside the door. His new classmates ran around the yard. They played in small groups, chasing hoops and tossing balls. He watched, too nervous to approach. Morning classes provided few opportunities to make friends, but the full yard was too daunting.

"Well, well, well! What do we have 'ere?"

Edward turned around to face a much larger boy. His blazer strained across his bulk, and acne peppered his pale skin. A mop of orange hair tumbled around his lumpy ears. The boy planted a squat hand on Edward's shoulder and steered him into the yard.

The games in the yard stopped. All eyes fell on Edward. He gulped at the sudden attention. A small blond boy to his right caught his eye. An ugly bruise coloured his cheekbone purple and blue. A pleading look haunted his eyes as he mouthed the word, "Run".

Other large boys peeled away from groups scattered across the yard. They formed a loose cordon around Edward and his guard. Edward sensed the other boys forming a wider ring. They struggled to see. Edward's hands shook, and a bead of ice cold sweat trickled down his forehead. It made his eye sting.

"You're the new boy, aren't you?"

The tallest boy looked down at him. Greasy black hair fell over his forehead into his dull grey eyes. The ghost of a scar twisted his face into a snarl.

"Yes, sir," replied Edward.

"He calls me sir!" said the older boy. He brayed, and the other boys added their own uneasy laughter to the chorus. The black-haired boy clapped his approval.

"You know your place. I like that. I can see that we're going to get along famously. But you can call me Simmers."

The laughter died away. Silence descended on the yard, Edward felt time slow to a crawl. He thought of his father, fighting the armies of Napoleon in the killing fields of northern Spain. If Papa could be brave, so could he.

"Do you know where you are?" asked Simmers.

"Ch-Ch-Charterhouse School," replied Edward.

"That's right. But do you know what was here before the school?"

Edward shook his head. The district of Clerkenwell confused him. London was too big to take in at once.

"Didn't reckon you would know, you being new, but that's alright. I'm here to tell you. This place was built on a plague pit. You know what they are?"

Edward nodded.

"Of course you do. Everyone knows about plague

pits. Only this one was especially despicable. They didn't always wait for you to die before they threw you in."

Edward stared at the older boy. He didn't want to believe him, but truth lay in the lines of his ugly face. Sadness gripped his heart. His father's tales of human cruelty echoed in his ears.

Two of the boys grabbed Edward's arms and forced him to the ground. Simmers pressed his head down, his right ear against the cold cobbles of the yard. He heard nothing except the silence of the watching boys. He wondered if the teachers could see. Would they care, even if they did see?

"Can you hear them? The cries of the ones they buried alive?"

Edward tried not to listen, his ears filled with pounding of blood. A cloud parted in the darkness, and a muffled sob reached through the veil of years. A sob, a wail, a plaintive plea. Edward gasped, but his lungs refused to breathe in. More cries, howls, and weeping added to the lament of the dead. They called his name, asking for help. They begged to be free.

Edward yelped and struggled, forcing himself up. Simmers fell back, his eyes wide. The two captors released his arms. Air rushed into Edward's lungs and a scream bubbled up in his throat. Terror forced the cry loose. The boys backed away in the face of naked despair.

Edward still howled when his geography master dragged him inside, away from the alarmed stares of the boys. He only fell silent an hour later through exhaustion. He passed out in the headmaster's office and his mother came for him twenty minutes later. She cradled her unconscious son on the way home.

The headmaster hauled the small blond boy into his office. The boy answered his questions about the Newcomer's Ordeal. The headmaster asked to see Simmers. The black-haired boy expressed admiration that Edward survived his ordeal, but sorrow that he would never forget those eternal cries.

Edward never returned to the Charterhouse School.

The Dead-House

None of the other nurses will venture into the ground floor corridor of the east wing at night. Not for all the jewels in the Prince Regent's storehouse, they say. Even Martin, the gruff old porter, avoids the corridor, although he claims it's because the chill in that part of the building plays havoc with his joints. Everyone else says it has more to do with the conversion of a disused ward into a new morgue, which everyone calls the 'dead-house'.

"But surely the dead-house is a good thing?" I used to ask. "It is good that we can determine the true cause of their death." I thought of my own father, whose death under suspicious circumstances could have been investigated, and his murderers brought to account.

"Nonsense, girl. You can't keep the dead from their

burial and then be surprised when they walk abroad," Matron would reply.

I don't understand such ideas, and I would have thought a woman of usual good sense and intelligence such as Matron would have dismissed them herself But in my three months at the hospital, I have learned not to disagree with or question Matron. It is true, my only experience of the dreaded corridor has been during the day, when light floods the passage through the windows that line the outside wall, but that is beside the point. It is only a morgue, and a corridor. How bad can they really be by night?

In December, my first night shift arrives. At first, the work is no different to usual, as the patients do not respect the chiming clock. They wander the corridors or call for help at any time of the night or day. Yet at a quarter to midnight, Matron asks me to visit a patient in the east wing. There are different routes through the hospital, but this is my chance to see exactly what everyone is so afraid of and a sort of mad curiosity propels me. I half-run through the labyrinth of the ground floor until I reach the corridor that everyone else dreads.

As I turn the corner into the passage, I still can't see why everyone so pointedly avoids this part of the hospital. Moonlight streams through the windows, casting shadows of the frames across the opposite wall. It is so peaceful – no one is here to moan or cry for help. Faint voices come from somewhere to my right, no doubt from beyond the wall, but I assume they belong to those working in the dead-house. No one ever speaks of the morticians, and I wonder what their opinion of this corridor is. They must surely know its reputation, yet they work there all the same. What are they like, spending so much of their time around the dead?

I am halfway along the corridor when a knock sounds behind me. I turn around, expecting to see one of the infirm patients struggling with a cane. This has happened before on many occasions, and I always tend to their needs and return them to their bed. Yet there is no one there. I shrug, and continue along the corridor. It runs the length of most of this wing, and it is longer than I remember it being during the day. It does not take this many steps at noon.

Another knock comes from behind me, and then another. I turn around again and still there is no one there. More knocks – it sounds as though someone raps on the wall. I am level with the doors to the dead-house, but the knocks do not come from inside. They are in the corridor – with me.

Unease grows in my chest, and I start walking again, this time a little faster than before. This time the knocks are harder and more insistent, and closer. They are following me along the corridor. I speed up, close to a brisk trot, and the knocks increase to match my pace. I half consider going back to the dead-house, thinking some human companionship may settle my nerves, but I do not want the morticians to think me simple or easily swayed by the folk tales of others.

I have a job to do, and I hurry towards the door at the end of the corridor. The knocks accompany me, and I resist all urges to look behind me. Surely there is nothing there, and if I had time to investigate, there would inevitably be a rational explanation. The world is a place of reason and science; this is merely a phenomenon of the latter. I must continue attending to my duties.

The door stands before me and I reach out to grasp the handle. Another knock sounds, this time from the other side of the door. I squeal, and stare at the knob, expecting to see it turn. I stand rooted to the spot for what feels like hours. There is a church across the fields on this side of the building, and its clock heralds midnight with a chiming bell. The witching hour is at hand. The sound, halfway between a chime and a knell, breaks the spell. Someone, or something, knocks on the door from the other side.

I run back along the corridor before the decision is completely made, and I reach the dead-house. Even if they think me a simpleton for asking, I am determined to question the morticians on their understanding of the knocks in this corridor. Their knowledge of science is so much more advanced than mine, after all. They investigate the secrets of life and death, and there is little they do not know.

Knocking pursues me along the corridor, and a second set of raps begins at the other end of the corridor, rushing toward me until I am caught between the sounds outside the morgue. I open the door and slip inside before my nerves can fail me.

I confess that I have never set foot inside a morgue before. How could I have done so, when this is my first nursing post in a city hospital, and the dead-house is a new invention? Yet even with my lack of experience, I know I am not where I want to be. This is not the dead-house – and I realise with a chill that I may not be in the hospital anymore.

A vaulted room lies before me, the green bloom of moss clinging to grey stone. Its ribbed ceiling and smell of age reminds me of the crypt of St Anne's, the small parish church where I played with my sisters as a child. We cared little for the rotting coffins. There are no caskets here, just bare walls and no windows. Unlit torches hang in wall brackets, and flickering shadows dance across the deeply pitted floor. I cannot see any source of illumination, or indeed anything to cast the shades that wheel and turn.

"Hello?" I call a greeting though I know that there are no morticians here. I just want to hear a human voice, even if it is my own.

I turn back to the doors, and I fall backwards in fright as a young man now stands between me and the way out of this place. He wears a fine frock coat of deep grey velvet that reminds me of smoke in a breeze, and a top hat of a black so deep it hurts my eyes to look at it. Spectacles rest on his nose, their round black lenses obscuring his eyes. I estimate he is perhaps twenty-five, and his broad smile provokes an unsettling combination of pleasure and dread in my stomach.

"Excuse me, sir, I must return to the hospital."

"Must you indeed? And why is that, my dear lady?" The young man bows deeply, though I cannot help thinking he is insulting me somehow.

"Matron will wonder where I am."

"She sent you on an errand?" The young man moves away from the door, and I cannot help following his progress further into the strange room.

"She did."

"Then I wonder at your venturing in here, if you're otherwise occupied."

I scowl at him. He has a point, but I cannot tell him about the knocking. I don't even know who he is.

"If you don't mind me asking, who are you, and what are you doing in the dead-house?" I know I'm not in the dead-house but it seems the only question to ask.

"Who am I? Well who are any of us, really? Which of us gives our true name, and who among us allows others to know the real us?" He laughs, amused by his own wit, although I cannot understand what he is getting at.

"Excuse me?"

"Never mind me, my dear lady. In answer to your second question, I am not in your dead-house. No, indeed you are in mine."

The shock must register upon my face because he swoops forward, and takes hold of my hands. He peers into my eyes as if appraising me for illness. His fingers are like ice in my grasp, yet I cannot pull myself free. He repulses and enchants me at the same time – if it were not an inappropriate reference, I would compare him to the operations that I have seen the surgeons perform. There is a grim beauty to their grisly machinations from which I cannot avert my gaze.

"Your dead-house, sir?"

"Indeed, dear! Come, let me show you around."

Before I can protest, he leads me further into the vaulted room, which turns out to be a corridor. A distinct chill hangs in the air, and I am left with the impression that we are somewhere below ground.

"What is this place?"

"I told you. It is my dead-house."

"But we are the only ones here." I am yet to hear or see anyone besides ourselves.

"Ha! How little you know, my dear lady." The young man will not be pressed further, and skips ahead, his fingers still entwined with mine. Our speed gives the impression of flight along the corridor, yet my mind rails against the assumption. How could we move faster than a run without breaking into a swift pace?

"I wish to know where I am!" I try to pull my hand free, and do my best to dig in my heels. I manage neither, but the young man stops all the same.

"I apologise, little one. You do not like this space?"

I frown, and without warning, he places his hand over my eyes. His skin is like ice, yet it also smells cold, damp with the cloying scent of the grave.

A second later, he removes his hand, and the vaulted corridor has gone. It is replaced with a vast meadow, tall wildflowers casting explosions of colour against the grass. A breeze ruffles their heads, though I feel nothing on my skin. Clouds scud across the blue sky that arcs above us, though something feels wrong. No bird song fills the air, and the sun's rays bear no warmth. It is as though I am walking in a painting, beautiful yet unreal. I expect to run my hands through the flowers and smear the colours.

"Are we still in your dead-house?"

"Indeed we are. Inside, or outside, it's all the same to me. Space is space, after all." The young man waves his hand around, gesturing to the meadow which stretches as far as I can see, as if this somehow answers my question.

"My dead-house, that is, the dead-house I was looking for, is a busy place. Morticians work to ascertain why people have died, if it is not immediately obvious. There are always cadavers, and I feel sure there must be equipment, and there are the morticians themselves..." I do not end my sentence, sure that he knows what I would like to ask.

"You want to know why I call this place my dead-house, when it so little resembles your own." The previous good humour drains from his expression, and his face is sketched in sharp, hard lines. For the first time I am glad I cannot see his eyes behind his impenetrable spectacles. I don't imagine I would like what I might find there.

"Exactly. You're clearly very proud of your dead-house, and it is very impressive. I just wanted you to help me to understand it better."

I sincerely hope my flattery sounds genuine, and he must detect a note of real curiosity in it, for he laughs, and softness returns to his face. He is both handsome in his looks and repulsive in his very air of 'wrong-ness', yet there is something addictive about his laugh, as though it could chase away melancholy and conjure genies.

"I am a mortician, of sorts. A mortician, and a musician. I too investigate the dead, and I lead them on such a merry dance!" He demonstrates a little jig, but his grin reminds me of the macabre woodcuts that my particularly morbid aunt would always bring out whenever I paid a visit. There is something of the goblin about him.

"I asked this earlier and you didn't answer my question, but I think I've been exceptionally patient, particularly when I have no idea where I am and why I'm not in the hospital any more. Exactly who are you?" I narrow my eyes and peer at him, as if this may strip away his façade and allow me to see who, or what, he really is. Many of my fellow nurses would have fainted clean away by now, but I fancy myself to be of hardier stock. Besides, this jaunt through a world that cannot possibly be real is still preferable to scrubbing bed pans.

"I go by many names, my dearest one. In fact, I have so many I cannot even remember which one was the first. But all you need worry yourself with at present is that you are in my dead-house, and I am the closest I think you will get to encountering a mortician."

He turns and skips away from me, the wildflowers bowing to provide him with a clear path. They spring back up behind him, leaving me to push my way through. They leave no pollen or fallen petals on my skirts, and I conclude that if I were to sniff one, I would smell nothing. I pinch the head from what I believe to be a poppy and slip it into my pocket, determined to examine it more closely when I return to the hospital. That is, *if* I return to the hospital.

"If this is a dead-house, then where are the dead?" I call after him, hoping that he can hear me above the abysmal tune he has begun whistle.

"They are all around you, my love." He calls over his shoulder to me, and pauses to allow me to catch up.

"I cannot see anything."

The young man frowns again, and places his hand over my eyes. This time I reach up, and my fingers fasten around his own, but the sensation is too unpleasant, and I let out a small whimper. The young man chuckles, and removes his hand, disentangling himself from my grasp. He appears as repulsed by my touch as I am by his.

The meadow is replaced by a lofty ballroom, its walls lined with mirrors. Candles nestle within the chandeliers, crystal droplets reflecting tiny flames as if the ceiling were crawling with fireflies. We are not alone – the ballroom is filled with hundreds, if not thousands, of men and women, all wearing elegant frock coats or magnificent dresses. The women wear their powdered wigs sculpted into fantastic forms, while the men wear more subtle wigs of delicate curls. I recognise this sort of garb from an earlier decade – these people look magnificent but they are ever so slightly out of date. They all wear masks, and their dead eyes peer towards me.

"Do not pretend that this is also your dead-house." I cannot stop myself from admonishing the young man, now dressed in a black frock coat, tri-corner hat and breeches. His spectacles have been replaced by a mask, yet I still cannot see his eyes.

"But of course it is. And you wanted to see the dead – here they are. Well, some of them. I couldn't possibly fit all of them in here."

The young man snaps his fingers and somewhere within the room a string quartet bursts into life. The crush of people surrounding me loses interest and I find myself among dancing couples too intent on intricate footwork to notice a young woman in a nurse's uniform. I dip and dodge to weave through the dancers to pursue the young man. I am tired of his finery and the scenes to which he would have me bear witness – I wish to return to work.

I find him standing beside a grand fireplace, in conversation with a young woman who bears an uncanny resemblance to the late wife of the hospital's patron. I tell him that I wish to leave.

"Leave? But you only just got here, my lovely one." He pours syrup onto his words but I am resolute.

"I am very grateful for the time you have spent with me, and I have seen some fascinating things, but I really should be getting back to work."

He looks at me, long and hard, and I can see a

raised eyebrow above his mask. He taps his chin with a gloved finger, and I know he has already resolved himself to allow me to leave – he merely wishes to prolong the suspense.

"There is one who would speak with you first."

"If it's all the same with you, I'd like to go back to work. Matron will string me up for this as it is."

"Then what will a few more moments cost?"

He moves away in his jaunty way, and I follow him. I do not see that I particularly have a choice in the matter – he has no intention of sending me on my way until he has had his fun. A woman dancing beneath the largest of the chandeliers drops her fan, and whirls away before I can stop her. I stoop and pick it up, adding it to the flower in my pocket. Surely these will be proof of my absence – and something to investigate once my shift has ended.

The young man stops so abruptly that I walk into him, and the weight of his glare almost crushes me. He swiftly recollects himself and stands aside, so that I may see this mysterious person who wishes to speak with me.

It is my father. Unlike the others, tall and elegant in their eternity, my father's skin is mottled, his eyes watery and blank, and the scent of the grave clings to his tattered burial suit. He looks at me, but there is no spark of recognition, no exclamation of joy. He merely stares. Revulsion sends shudders through me, and my stomach heaves..

It is too much for my mind. I have been able to comprehend the ceaseless corridor, the painted meadow, and the grand ballroom as being figments of an imagination – not necessarily mine, but clearly someone's – but this is beyond my ken. All of the questions I had about my father's death are swallowed by confusion and sadness. Grief and despair collide, and tears spring to my eyes. Without speaking a word, I turn and flee, plunging across the room as fast as I can go. The dancers part for me, allowing me past. I dare not look at them, fearing that they will have taken on the same appearance as my father. The illusion has cracked, and I no longer want to see.

I reach the double doors at the far end of the room. They are the same as the doors that lead into the dead-house in the hospital. I grasp the handle and turn, but the door does not give. I rattle the knob, and release a string of profanities that might curl the toes of the most seaworthy sailor. I glance in the mirror, and see the dancers continuing their macabre dance. Their reflections remain glorious.

The young man appears at my side, no longer in his finery, but clad once more in the outfit he wore when first we met. The ballroom disappears, replaced by the vaulted room in which I first encountered him.

"You were not pleased to see your father."

"Would you have been, to see a loved one so decrepit?"

"I have never had parents, so I couldn't possibly imagine. I assume you want to leave now."

I glare at him with all of the hatred and anger that I can muster, but he merely laughs off my abhorrence and leans against the door frame.

"Why can I not open the door?"

"This door only opens one way. You may enter through it, but you cannot leave. Except on one very special occasion."

"And what's that? Halloween?" I spit at his feet, convinced he is as possessed by morbid superstition as the idiots that I work with.

"Not at all. You heard the knocking, but you did not ask the right question before you came in here."

"And what question is that?"

"Oh you've heard it a thousand times, I expect. Knock knock –"

"Who's there?" I mumble my reply, astonished that I have been outwitted by a tedious joke.

"Indeed." The young man makes a show of removing a silver pocket watch from his waistcoat, and checking the time. I fear he will grow bored with me before I can find out how to leave this place.

"Am I dead?"

"Not really, no. You're not alive, but you're not dead."

"I don't understand. I'm getting so tired of your riddles and half-truths!" Anger clenches my hand into a fist, and I slam the door behind me. The pain blossoms and the tears that earlier filled my eyes finally spill free. The young man looks alarmed and hands me a handkerchief. An elaborate skull is embroidered upon one corner. I dab at my eyes, grateful that at least my tears are real, but the motif does not reassure me.

"The dead-house of which you speak is an in-between place. The dead are not truly dead until they are buried, but nor are they alive. My dead-house operates along the same lines, and the boundary is not so permanent. My door swings both ways, as it were." He rests a hand upon my shoulder but I am too upset to recoil. His touch is oddly comforting, even if his presence continues to unsettle me.

"It does? So how do I get back?"

"Keep knocking. When someone asks the right question, you can go."

With that, he is gone. He takes with him the vaulted room, and leaves me sitting on a beach. The doors remain, halfway between the sea and the sand dunes, and I rest against them, enjoying their solidity. The sky is a washed-out grey, full of the promise of an evening storm, and twisted driftwood is scattered across the sand. I recognise the beach, having played on it every afternoon during my childhood. No wind lifts my hair, and the air does not smell of salt, but I'm sure I shall be happy enough here.

I remain seated for a little while longer, lost in

my memories, until I remember what the young man said. I pull myself up and stand at the door. I make a fist, and knock. Once, twice, three times...as many times as it takes to get an answer.

Meeting Oneself

It happened on a bitter morning, beset by the sort of cold that you only feel in the dark days before Christmas. I had business in town, and rose early so as to conclude my transactions by a reasonable hour. The house was mostly in darkness, with a single maid trudging between the rooms to light fires in the grates. When I bade her good morning, she looked at me as though she had seen a ghost, and dropped her kindling on the parlour floor.

"Good God, girl, whatever is the matter?" I asked. I was especially surprised as I had not known Elsie to be a fanciful or superstitious creature in the eight months she had worked for me.

"Begging yer pardon, sir, I thought you was someone else." She bent to gather her parcel of wood and paper.

"Who?"

Elsie looked up at me, a somewhat thoughtful expression on her face.

"I din't listen at first, sir, though all the girls was talking about it. But I seen it for myself now."

"What? What did you see?"

"Yer ghost, sir." Elsie replied with no trace of amusement. The girl was deadly serious.

"My ghost?"

"That's right, sir. The other girls thought it was you at first, but then Sally saw it in the kitchen when we knew you was in the dining room with Mr Hardcastle."

I remembered the incident – Hardcastle and I were enjoying dinner when a scream interrupted our hearty conversation. I hurried to discover the source of the cry, but found the kitchen empty. I presumed it to have not been a scream, but rather the cry of some wild animal outside, and dinner continued once more. I had thought of it no more until Elsie raised the subject.

"But I live, Elsie, as you can see for yourself. I would need to be dead to have a ghost."

"Begging yer pardon, sir, but my mother says the living have ghosts too. They pass on messages then they leave."

I shuddered, considering the possibility of a version of myself that was dead yet somehow invading my home. I caught the earnest expression on Elsie's face and shook the mood from myself.

"Don't be absurd, Elsie. I have no ghost – there are no spirits in this house. Now run along and finish your jobs before Mrs Peterson awakes."

Elsie bobbed in an awkward curtsey and scurried away. The thought of my abrupt housekeeper no doubt scared her more than some silly ghost story.

I left the parlour, intending to visit my library before I left for town. I stood at the head of the long, narrow corridor that led to the back of the house. Little light pervaded its pre-dawn gloom, and I shivered. I debated with myself for several moments about the importance of the papers for my business in town, before mentally shaking myself. I had allowed myself to become unnerved by an idle report, given by a maid, no less. No, it would not do. I plunged into the darkness in the direction of my library.

I opened the door and the sight almost stopped my heart.

My double stood in the centre of the library, the weak dawn rays falling through the figure onto the carpet. I looked closer and saw that it was not quite the double of myself – the right side of its face was horribly burned, contorted into an expression of the purest pain. My hand flew to my own face, my fingers exploring the skin, yet finding it marred by nothing but stubble.

The figure reached out a hand and opened its mouth, its lips forming silent words. I could not make them out, but felt perhaps they were a warning of some kind. The double took two steps toward me, and vanished into the cold morning air. Before I could consider what the apparition might signify, I fell into a faint, and dropped to the floor.

I awoke some six hours later, with my brother in my room and the doctor scratching his illegible symbols into his notebook.

"Edgar! You return to us!" My brother strode to my bedside and peered into my face.

"Indeed I do. What time is it?" The memory of my intended meeting in town returned to me before that of the figure in the library.

"It is eleven in the morning."

"I was supposed to meet with Fitzherbert three hours ago!"

"Well you shan't be meeting with him at all now." My brother crossed himself, and briefly bowed his head. The doctor, despite his scientific allegiances, did likewise.

"What has happened?"

"A fire claimed Fitzherbert's house in town this morning. His business associates were able to escape but Fitzherbert did not have their good fortune. God rest his soul."

I thought of the many other instances when I had avoided some misfortune or other by being somewhere other than where I was supposed to be at that moment, and I fell into a faint for the second time that day.

Credits

'Black Dog' was first published in Sanitarium #44.

'A Woman of Disrepute' was first published in the Suspended in Dusk anthology.

'Midnight Screams at Holborn' was originally published in Bloody Parchment: Blue Honey and The Valley of Shadow.

'Something Wicked This Way Slithered' was originally published in Bloody Parchment: Beachfront Starter Home, Good Bones.

'The Cursed One' was originally published in European Monsters.

'The Jar by the Door' was originally published in Masks.

'The Dead-House' was originally recorded for the Tales to Terrify podcast.

'Meeting Oneself' was originally published in Literary Hatchet #9.

Did you enjoy *Black Dog & Other Gothic Tales*? Don't forget to leave a review on your favourite retailer's website – even if it's only short. It helps readers find better books to read from online stores.

Thank you!

At the start of this book, I promised you a complimentary story collection. So if you enjoyed this book, and you'd like a free copy of my previous collection, *Harbingers: Dark Tales of Speculative Fiction,* then join my mailing list!

Go to;
http://www.icysedgwick.com/harbingers/
to get your free copy.

You'll also get one monthly email (I'm not a spam factory, after all) containing a free short story, book recommendations, and other cool stuff I think you might like.

Don't worry that I'll just bombard you with "BUY MY BOOK!" That isn't my style.

But if you sign up, you'll also get the chance to join my review team, which means you get free copies of my books before they're released, and all you have to do is pop a short review on Amazon!

Meet the Author

Icy Sedgwick was born in the north east of England, and is currently based in Newcastle. She had her first book, the pulp Western adventure, *The Guns of Retribution*, published in September 2011. When she isn't writing or teaching, she's working on a PhD in Film Studies, knitting, exploring graveyards, or watching history documentaries.

Connect with Icy

Website:
http://www.icysedgwick.com/

Twitter:
https://twitter.com/IcySedgwick/

Instagram:
https://www.instagram.com/icysedgwick/

Facebook:
https://www.facebook.com/miss.icy.sedgwick/

Pinterest:
https://www.pinterest.co.uk/icysedgwick/

G+:
https://plus.google.com/+IcySedgwick/about

Printed in Great Britain
by Amazon

57817988R00069